GW00480665

ANARCHY

Other titles by James Robert Baker available from Alyson Books

Tim and Pete
Adrenaline
Testosterone

ANARCHY

A Novel by James Robert Baker

Edited by Scott Brassart

MANUFACTURED IN THE UNITED STATES OF AMERICA.

THIS TRADE PAPERBACK ORIGINAL IS PUBLISHED BY ALYSON PUBLICATIONS,
P.O. BOX 4371, LOS ANGELES, CALIFORNIA 90078-4371.
DISTRIBUTION IN THE UNITED KINGDOM BY
TURNAROUND PUBLISHER SERVICES LTD.,
UNIT 3, OLYMPIA TRADING ESTATE, COBURG ROAD, WOOD GREEN,
LONDON N22 6TZ ENGLAND.

FIRST EDITION: APRIL 2002

02 03 04 5 6 a 10 9 8 7 6 5 4 3 2 1

ISBN 1-55583-743-3

COVER DESIGN BY MATT SAMS.
COVER PHOTOGRAPHY BY LORENZO GOMEZ.

PART ONE
MEAN BEACH

It was a beautiful day, a hot summer day, and I was finishing off my workout with 200 sit-ups when the phone rang.

"Yeah, what?"

"Jim?"

"Yeah."

"Jim Baker?"

"Yeah."

"Linkletter, LAPD."

"*Art* Linkletter?"

"Frank Linkletter. *Detective* Frank Linkletter."

I wiped the sweat from my chest and stomach, and wondered what I'd done.

"We've got a hostage situation," he said. "A *serious* hostage situation, and I think you might be able to help."

"What makes you think I can help?"

"We've got some teenage geek down here at Will Rogers Beach with an AK-47. He's holding 21 *Sea Crew* extras hostage in a snack bar. Threatening to kill them all unless we let him have sex with movie stars."

I still didn't understand what this had to do with me, but it sounded interesting. "Movie stars?" I said. "Like who?"

"Like Brad Pitt and Johnny Depp."

"So the kid's gay?"

"A safe assumption. We found a paperback of your book in his car."

I assumed correctly that he meant my anarcho-queer novel *Tim and Pete*, which deals in part with a gang of AIDS-infected terrorists plotting to kill right-wing politicians. To be honest, I'd half hoped the book would inspire someone to assassinate, say, Jesse Helms. But I'd never even remotely wanted or expected to inspire some poor, hurting homo to take up arms against the hard-bodied dim bulbs of *Sea Crew*.

It occurred to me that this might be one of my friends playing a joke, but Linkletter felt like a true-to-life LAPD asshole. And I'd met enough of them to know. "OK," I told him. "I'll be there in 15 minutes."

At the time, I was living in Topanga Canyon in a wood and plate-glass house with a stupendous view of the chaparral covered Santa Monica Mountains. I pulled on a pair of ragged jeans and a faded T-shirt, and blasted down the winding canyon road to the state beach along Pacific Coast Highway, where I saw the cluster of *Sea Crew* trucks and trailers, along with maybe 20 black-and-whites and a SWAT team in full gear, set up to take the kid out with a laser-scoped round if he showed his head.

I picked out Linkletter right away—a booze-battered Ned Beatty with a badly dyed shit-brown comb-over—and introduced myself.

"He's got 'em in there," said the bedraggled detective. He indicated a faded blue stucco snack bar building. "We've got him on TV," he added, pointing to one of the trailers. "They were filming in the snack bar with a video replay deal."

"Where's his car?" I asked.

"Honda Civic." Linkletter pointed to the beat-to-shit late-'70s car.

I checked it out. Ripped upholstery, a dog-eared copy of *Tim and Pete,* and cassette tapes. Some current stuff like Moby and Korn, and, most tellingly, virtually the complete works of Morrissey: all of The Smiths' tapes and Morrissey's solo works, up through *Your Arsenal.* So we had a Morrissey freak on our hands.

"OK," I said to Linkletter. "Can I talk to him?"

"Over the phone. In the trailer."

I stepped into the trailer, which was packed with video equipment. And there he was on several color monitors. Maybe 19, skinny, red hair, thick glasses. Geeky, you could say, but not irrevocably butt-ugly. Here was a very lonely boy, a loveless and deeply frustrated masturbator. Trembling as he covered the group of scantily clad extras: shirtless muscle boys and big-breasted bimbos in thong bikinis. They were also trembling.

"What's his name?" I asked Linkletter.

"Billy Seavers."

I took the phone. "Billy?"

"Brad?" His voice was wary and high-pitched. He was on

something. Speed, I guessed. "Is that you, Brad?"

"No, Billy. This is James Robert Baker."

That took a moment to register. Then it rattled him. "What are *you* doing here? I don't want to fuck *you*. I've seen your picture. You're not bad, but you're old. I want to fuck Brad Pitt."

"Who doesn't?" I said, wondering if 36 qualified as old. "But Brad's unavailable."

Linkletter mouthed, "Argentina."

"He's on location in Argentina," I said, fairly certain I was lying.

"I don't care," Billy whined. "I want him here. Even if it takes hours. I want to have sex with him. Otherwise all these airheads are gonna die."

"You don't like them, do you?" I said evenly.

"I hate them. They're all so perfect." Bitter rage twisted his voice. "Perfect bodies. Perfect faces. Perfect, perfect, *perfect*! But they're morons with big tits and muscles and room-temperature IQs."

"Lookism," I said.

"Lookism?"

"Judging people by their outward appearance. You've been oppressed by that, haven't you, Billy? People rejecting you and treating you like shit just because you're not a vapid muscle boy."

"So."

"So that's how you just rejected me." I admit, I was grasping here. "You liked my novel, I could tell. It's dog-eared. But you're not interested in me sexually because I'm past a certain age. How do you think that makes me feel? I'd say you're just as guilty of lookism as anyone else."

"Who cares?" he said coldly. "I don't have to be consistent. I don't have to be anything. And I don't have to talk to you. Or the cops. I'm calling the shots here. That's the whole point. For the first time in my life, *I'm* calling the shots. And if Brad really is in Argentina, which I doubt, but if he is, then I want to fuck Johnny Depp."

"Unreachable," mouthed Linkletter.

"We've haven't been able to reach him." I said. "He may be out on a binge. We don't know for sure." Deliberate pause. "But we *have* patched through a call from Manchester, England. From someone who'd like to talk to you."

"England?" said Billy.

Linkletter looked at me like I was crazy. I shrugged. I knew he wouldn't have called in a civilian if he wasn't desperate.

"Hello, Billy?" I said in a Manchester accent. (I do accents. You'd be surprised how often this comes in handy.)

I saw him on the monitor, reacting as if he knew who I was—who I was supposed to be—even before I identified myself.

"Billy," I said. "This is Morrissey. I hear you've got yourself in some trouble, my friend."

"Morrissey?" he said. And even though the monitor picture was a wide shot, I'm pretty sure I saw his eyes well up. "Is that really you?"

"Yes, it is, mate. I'm calling from my home here in Manchester, Billy, because I hear you're in trouble."

"Morrissey?" His voice broke. "Is that really, really you?"

"It's really me, Billy."

He suddenly stiffened. "How do I know this isn't a trick?"

"It's not a trick, Billy. I'm truly concerned about you."

"Sing 'Suedehead,' " he said sharply. "If you're really Morrissey, you'll know the words."

I covered the mouthpiece and told Linkletter to get the cassettes from Billy's car, praying they included the lyric sheets. To buy time, I told Billy, "That's an old song. I was in an odd frame of mind when I wrote it. I don't sing it in concert anymore. I'm not certain if I remember how it goes."

"I don't see how you could forget a song that personal," Billy said, just as Linkletter returned with the cassettes.

I opened *Viva Hate,* and, thank God, there was a lyric sheet.

"You're right," I told Billy. "It was a very personal song." I sang the first verse, which I'm not going to quote here, since I don't want to pay a permission fee. But it worked. It worked so convincingly that Billy began to cry.

"Morrissey!" he wailed. "I'm so scared! I fucked up so bad, but I didn't know what else to do. I'm still a virgin."

"There are worse things than being celibate," I said.

"I'm not talking about celibacy," Billy sobbed. "That implies you've had sex and then given it up. *I've never had it!* I've never sexually touched another human being!"

I really felt for him at this point, which made it easier to stay in character. "I know, Billy. I've been scared too. Which is why I understand. I think perhaps we have some sort of spiritual connection. It's as though you know my dark side."

"What do you mean?"

"I mean, without a creative outlet, I might be where you are now. I hate the way people treat each other as objects, as *things.* I understand your anger at the *Sea Crew* lot. They epitomize the superficial values that have kept both you and I so alone."

"I know," Billy said. "That's why I'm going to kill them. Because they're everything I hate."

"But Billy, don't you see? If you do that, they'll have won. You'll be written off as a psychopath driven jealously insane by their superficial beauty."

"But what else can I do?" Billy wailed.

"You can surrender," I said, "to James Robert Baker. He's a brilliant writer who truly does understand. You haven't killed anyone yet, have you?"

"No, but I almost killed Ronnie Kessler." The show's aging pretty-boy star. "I saw him in his trailer and I had a clear shot. But I was looking for Patti Grant. I was going to just grab her. That was my original plan. But she's not here. She didn't have any scenes today."

I'd wondered why he hadn't gone for Grant, certainly the planet's most famous bad actress, with a Barbie body and a gleam in her eye as faint as a courtesy light.

"I wanted her as my sole hostage," Billy cried. "Instead I had to settle for these dumb-ass Patti Grant wannabes. And I'm getting *very tired* of listening to them whimper."

"Then surrender," I said. "To James. You'll be treated as a psychological case. You'll undergo treatment. During which time, I promise you, I shall come and visit."

"You'll come and see me?"

"Yes. We shall speak through a glass wall, no doubt. Or maybe not. Maybe they'll let us sit in a bare room, where I can reach across the table and take your hands in mine. And eventually you will be released, my troubled lad. And then..."

"Then?"

"And then we shall see. I shan't make false promises. So

many fans have tried so many different times in so many different ways to beguile me into breaking my celibacy. But I don't place you among those tricksters." I paused. "Billy, I cannot promise you my physical love, but I *do* feel a spiritual connection. I know the pain you're enduring. I know the time will come when you will be well and released into society. And *I will be there* when you are. And I know that at the very least I'll want to put my arms around you and kiss you, however lightly, on the lips. More than that I cannot say. I have such fear myself."

To cut to the chase—and this took more time and talk—Billy surrendered. He put down his AK-47 and came outside to me. Whereupon the cops promptly grabbed him. I stood by as they handcuffed him and roughed him up. He was so pitiful that I couldn't bring myself to reveal the ruse. Instead, as they hustled him off to a cop car, I assured him Morrissey would be in close touch.

Needless to say, rcports of the *Sea Crew* incident were squelched or completely minimized. Not surprising, when you think about it. Hollywood is *very* sensitive—with cause—about anything that might inspire yet another psycho to act out.

I didn't mind. *Sea Crew* is a crappy show, and I didn't want to be labeled as the fag who saved it. Still, I'd rescued 21 people, and it would've been nice to get *something* out of it. Which is why I agreed to meet Linkletter at a crummy bar in South Gate. After downing a double Stoli, he burped and got to the point. "We have reason to believe there may be a tape of the Simpson murders."

"Come again?"

"You heard me," he said. "We have reason to believe that a witness, an eyewitness, made a videotape of the murders of Nicole Simpson and Ron Goldman. And that the tape shows the perpetrator as the Juice in no uncertain terms."

"Whoa."

"Want more?"

"What do you think?"

"The tape was made by a neighbor. A guy who lived, and still lives, across the street. He heard shouts and so forth and picked up his camcorder and taped the whole thing. Beginning to end."

"Jesus."

"As you might presume, we only learned of this recently. If we'd known about this before the trial... Although with that jury, who knows?"

"You've seen the tape?"

"No. That's the problem."

"What? Wait. Back up. There's an *alleged* tape, made by a neighbor, which you say *we* only learned of recently. Who's *we*? And how did *we* learn about the tape?"

Linkletter took a deep breath. "All right, here's the story. And let me start by saying that if you fuck me, I'll fuck you. *Comprende?*"

"Yeah, yeah. Get on with it."

"This neighbor, now he's somebody we knew of before. He was interviewed right after the crime. Said he was sleeping, didn't hear a thing. Nothing unusual. Same thing we got from lots of other neighbors. Either asleep or watching TV. Now, I didn't do that interview, since I wasn't on the case. But the detective who did made a note that...OK, here's his name. He made a note that Mr. *Kandinsky* seemed nervous. Or more to the point, that he might be withholding something. So there was a second visit, several weeks later. And this time Kandinsky was really nervous. But by now, who wouldn't be? It's the crime of the century, the media's all over it. But he still said he was asleep. So what are we gonna do? Take him downtown and use the rubber hose?"

"I guess you guys don't do that anymore, huh?"

He shrugged. "Not since Watts. It was never the same after that."

"Yeah, the '60s screwed up everything. So what happened?"

"Kandinsky called us. Last Friday. Said he had something to tell us about the case. But he wouldn't talk on the phone, so we drove out to Brentwood."

"Kandinsky? Polish?"

"No, Russian. He's a Russian national. Which is part of our problem. I'll get to that in a minute. So here's what happens. My partner and I get there, and Kandinsky lets us in. He's nervous. Real nervous. And he tells us he made this tape of the murders. While his wife was in the bedroom in the back of the house, watching TV. He says he'd been back there with her, when he went to the kitchen for a glass of milk or what-have-you. Heard an angry voice across the street. Looked out the window. Saw people standing by the condo gate having some kind of argument. But they were too far away for him to see that well. That's why he picked up his camcorder, which he'd used that afternoon on a visit to his sister-in-law in

Orange County. He figured he could use the zoom like binoculars. That was his first intention, anyway. Until he saw what was going on. That's when he pressed Record."

"But he didn't show you the tape?"

"He wouldn't. Not unless we paid him."

"He tried to extort you?"

"I believe that's the proper term."

"Jesus Christ. The guy's got balls."

"What he's got is diplomatic immunity."

"What? He's the Russian consul?"

"Not the consul. But he works there. He's a consulate official. He's covered. So you see our dilemma."

"How much does he want?

"Twenty-five grand. And that's just to *look* at the tape and give us a dub."

"Christ."

"Naturally, he tells us the tape's not on the premises and that it's well hidden."

"So where do I fit in?"

"I'll get to that," said Linkletter. "But first I want to show you these." He reached into his briefcase and pulled out a dirty manila folder. "Right as we're leaving, Kandinsky says, 'Just in case you think I'm bluffing...' and he hands us these." Linkletter looked around the bar to make sure no one was watching us, then opened the folder. In it were two glossy 8-by-10 color photos. Blurry stills that looked like they were made from the frames of a videotape. The light in both was yellowish, but the action depicted was clear enough. In the first, a man in a dark warm-up suit was stabbing a cornered Ron Goldman, who had his hands up in a futile attempt to stave off the attack. In the second and by far more shocking photo, the same man knelt over Nicole Simpson, who lay on the ground. With one gloved hand he pulled her head back by the hair. With the other hand, which was gloveless, he used the short knife to slit her throat. In the first shot the attacker wore a knit cap. In the second it was gone—as if he'd lost it in the struggle with Goldman. In both photos the attacker's face was exposed to the yellow streetlight. And the attacker was very clearly Orenthal James Simpson. In the second photo, he was facing the camera dead-on, baring his teeth like an animal going in for the kill.

"Fucking Christ," I whispered.

"I know."

I took a mental step back to think things through, to look at the photos again. They were, as I said, blurry. Just as you'd expect from a camcorder tape blowup. But they looked real. They looked exactly like what they were alleged to be: two frames pulled from a fast-action sequence captured on videotape.

Still, I knew what was possible with modern software programs. It would take much more than a naked-eye examination of the stills, and of the tape itself, if it existed, to validate their authenticity. It would take a microscopic examination of the pixels—and even then a well-executed forgery could be very hard to detect. To fake a tape, of course, would be much more difficult and time-consuming. But not as difficult as it was even a few years ago. Movie special effects created on computer, *Jurassic Park* for instance, could be made to look extremely real. And it's been a few years since *Jurassic Park.*

"I'd really like to see that tape," I told Linkletter.

"You and most of the world, if they knew about it."

I asked once again: "Why do you need me?"

"We want you to negotiate with the guy."

"Negotiate what? A better price?"

"No," he said, closing the manila folder. "If a tape exists, it could be a fake. And we can't tell shit from a dub. We need the original. You can start by offering 50 grand, and you can go up to a hundred. Let *him* keep the dub."

"Have the photos been examined?" I asked.

"Are you kidding? By who? Something like this would leak in minutes. I wish I *did* know someone I could trust."

"I may know someone," I said.

"I figured you would. I know your background is film. That's why I called you. Plus I'm a cop, and it would look bad if I was involved and something went wrong, right? Anyway, screw these fucking pictures. Get the tape and have your pal look at *that.* And make sure he keeps his mouth shut. There's 10 grand in it for you, plus whatever's left of the hundred after you pay Vlad."

"Vlad. Why am I not eager to meet a guy named Vlad?"

Linkletter pulled out his notebook and tore off a page with an address and phone number written on it. "He's expecting you. Don't keep him waiting."

"How are you going to get me the cash?"

"It's in the trunk of my car." He held up his hand. "Don't ask."

I didn't.

That night I called Vladimir Kandinsky, who indeed was expecting to hear from me. He had a thick Russian accent, and he sounded nervous as we made awkwardly cryptic plans for me to drop by his place the next evening. I had a sense he felt his phone was tapped. Perhaps it was.

I spent most of that night wondering what, if anything, the LAPD would do with the tape if in fact it existed and was verifiably real (or at least not verifiably fake). Release it to the media to prove they were right? Or destroy it to save themselves from further embarrassment? The latter seemed more likely. And what about the $100,000? Who fronted that and why? Even in a town like L.A., that's a pretty big chunk of change. And then it occurred to me: $100,000 is a pretty hefty sum, but it's pocket money compared to what the tape might fetch on the open market.

I tried in vain to make sense of it.

Finally, around dawn, I gave up, deciding I was too intrigued to back out and that the situation would work itself out as it went along. I washed down a pair of Valium with a tumbler of Jack Daniel's and went to sleep.

I reached Brentwood the next night at 7 o'clock. It was summer, so it was still light out. I rang Vlad's bell and he opened the door. He was about 40, with dirty-blond hair. The first word that came to my mind was *juicehead.* He had the look. His face, never handsome, was battered from the bottle. I could also smell it on his breath as he let me in.

It looked as if he'd lived there a while. The place was messy, the decor an odd combination of ugly heavy Soviet furniture mismatched with newer IKEA and Pier 1 stuff. He was still dressed from work, jacket off, tie loosened. He offered me a vodka, which I accepted, and he poured himself another one. Cheap American vodka.

"Do you have the money?" he said.

I opened the satchel and showed him the bundles of bills. I'd been listening carefully for anyone else in the house, but I had a strong sense we were alone. I wondered where his wife was.

He looked at the money. "This is more than I asked for. I don't understand."

"Well, here's the thing, Vlad," I said. "Is that what people call you? Vlad? Or Vladimir?"

"Vlad is fine."

"Here's the deal. Linkletter needs the *original.* Not a dub. That's the only way to verify the tape's authenticity."

"This was not our agreement."

"I know. That's why I brought the extra money. It's $50,000, Vlad. For the original tape." I had the other 50 in the trunk.

This threw him more than I'd expected. "OK, I would do this," he said finally. "For this kind of money, I would sell you the first tape. But I don't have it."

"You mean, it's not on the premises. I understand that—"

"No, no. I mean I don't have it anymore. I don't have it, period. My wife, she has it."

"And where is she?"

"I don't know." He was up and pacing at this point, which made me uneasy.

"You don't know."

"She left me. Last week. That's why I call Linkletter. Because I need money."

"You're losing me," I said. "Why don't you sit down and we'll have another drink and you can start at the beginning. With the murders."

"I don't have to sit down." He poured himself another glass. "I can tell you everything that happened. My wife was in the bedroom. Back there. I came out here for a bite of food and heard voices. Over there."

I looked out the window at the now-altered entrance to Nicole Simpson's old condo. (The new owners had put up a high wall and a solid gate to block the view of where the victims were found.) I was surprised by how close it really was. And it was twilight now. The yellow streetlights had come on.

"So I pick up the camera," he said, "to get a better look. That is when I see Nicole. And the other man, Goldman. And O.J."

"You recognized Nicole?"

"Oh, yes. We had spoken. Only briefly. But I would see her sometimes when she walked her dog."

"And you recognized O.J. too?"

"Yes. Yes, I knew who he was instantly. I had seen him here many times."

"When he visited Nicole?"

"Yes. Then and when he was spying."

"Spying?"

"I would see him on the sidewalk. I knew his truck, the famous Bronco. The first time, months before, I thought he was waiting. You know, for Nicole to come home. But then I looked again and saw him in the bushes, peering into her window. There was a dim light inside, like from candles. So I know he was spying."

"But you never called the police?"

"No," he shrugged. "Not when I saw it was him. If it had been a stranger, yes, of course. But I felt it was something between the two of them. I knew he sometimes spent the night with her. His truck would be there in the morning. You understand? It was something between the two of them. I did not wish to get involved."

"I see."

"One time I hear them argue at her gate. He called her a bitch. But then he stayed the night. You understand what I am saying?"

"I think so."

"And then this night of the murders, at first they only argue. Nicole and O.J. And this man who was Goldman. Then suddenly he stabbed her and I could not believe it."

"He stabbed her first?"

"Yes. Very fast. Then he turned on the other. You know what happened. I don't have to tell you. It was very bad. But it was not like they said at the trial, the way one man said. It did not take many minutes. It was over very quickly. He stabbed the man, Goldman, against the fence. And then he went back to Nicole and cut her throat. Just like they said. I saw it all. It's all on the tape."

At this point I was shaken. "Why didn't you call the police?"

"My wife stop me. 'Don't get involved,' she said. 'Someone else will call.' I thought she was right, that they would be here any second. But they did not come for two, three hours."

"What did you do during all that time? How could you not call the police? I mean, how did you know they weren't still alive?"

He shook his head. "They were quite still." His hands were

shaking as he poured himself yet another drink. "You must understand, where I come from...it is best to not be involved with the police."

"Same here," I said.

He tossed back his drink and continued. "Of course, they finally did arrive. Many police. Many. We shut out the lights so they would not know we were awake. Then I went to use the bathroom, and one came to the door."

"A cop?"

"Yes. He saw the bathroom light, so no more pretending. He knocked at the door quite hard. 'LAPD. Open, please.' So my wife open the door. He was police, but not in uniform."

"A detective?"

"Yes."

"Do you remember which one?"

"He ask my wife for a bag."

"A bag?"

"You know, plastic. Like for sandwich. He said to my wife, 'I need put this in bag.'"

"What was *this*?"

"A glove. A bloody leather glove."

"What? You're making this up."

"No. So my wife get him the bag. He takes it, puts the glove in the bag. He leaves. That's it. Until much later."

"Later?"

"Yes. He comes back, maybe two weeks later, with another man in uniform. They do this during the day, when I am at work. They tell my wife if she ever speaks of this glove, bad things will happen to her and to me. You understand?"

"Did this detective have blow-dried hair?"

"Please. You don't need me to answer this question."

"No, I guess not."

"After that, I hide the tape. I want no involvement."

"It *did* occur to you how crucial the tape might have been in court?"

"Of course. But I thought they would convict him without it. Again, where I come from... When the verdict came in, I was quite shocked."

"So why come clean now?"

"I need the money. You have heard of Gardena?"

"Sure," I said. "You mean you have gambling debts?"

"Yes. But not from legal blackjack parlors. From a private game. One night I drank too much and lost too much. In the private home of a Samoan. First he threaten my wife. This is why she has disappeared."

"Well," I said, "this just gets messier by the second." I stared across the street, imagined the blood on the sidewalk and the neighbors who first spotted the bodies while walking their dog. I formulated a strategy. "OK, look," I said. "Is that the only reason your wife split? I mean, does she still love you?"

"Of course. She's mad at me, but I know she still loves me. She is just afraid. He told her if I don't pay by this weekend, his men will smash her knees and cut up her face."

"OK. Well, let me ask you, do you have any idea where she might be? Any idea at all?"

"I have some guesses. She has relatives and friends in Orange County."

"Because if you can fork over the tape, the original, I can give you this money to pay off your debts. Is this enough to cover your debts?"

"I need $25,000 right away, but I owe $65,000 altogether."

"OK, $65,000 for the tape. So I suggest we find your wife. Quickly. Today's Wednesday. When will the Samoans be back?"

"Saturday."

"Call in sick tomorrow. So we can start looking for your wife."

He hesitated, but not for long. He glanced at the satchel and said, "OK."

"In the meantime, just so I know this isn't a load of crap, I think you should give me the dub."

"For $25,000."

"No. Vlad, listen. You're not hearing me. The dub is worthless, except as some indication as to whether this is bullshit or not. We need the original. I'm trying to save you, both you and your wife. So give me the dub, all right? I want to take it with me and watch it at home, where I can look at it carefully. I'll bring it back tomorrow. If it looks good, we'll go find your wife. That's the way it's got to be. Otherwise, no deal."

He sighed. "OK. Wait here."

I sat while he went out the back door, to the garage or the backyard or wherever he'd hidden the dub. Apparently, he'd buried it, since he came back with a dirty plastic trash bag, from which he produced a Sony VHS videocassette. Astonishingly, it was labeled with a felt pen: "Juice Murder." He handed it to me.

"OK," I told him. "I'm going to leave now. I'll watch this as soon as I get home and then I'll call you to let you know what I think. We'll take it from there, all right?"

He shrugged. "You have me on a barrel. I will think hard about where to look for my wife. Because I will tell you this: You will not be disappointed."

"We'll see. How long does the tape run?"

"Four minutes."

"OK. I'll call you in a while."

I didn't feel safe going home carrying that much cash and a tape of the most notorious murder of my generation, so I called my friend Rachel, a studio set designer. An hour after that we were opening the sofa bed in the guest room at her cottage in the Hollywood hills.

I told Rachel as little as possible, and she didn't ask questions, understanding she would likely be happier not knowing. This is a quality of Rachel's that I greatly admire, if only because I myself have no such restraint.

When she left me, I turned on the TV and VCR. Took the "Juice Murder" cassette from its box, and slipped it in. Found the remote.

Stretched out on the sofa bed, propped against the pillows, I wondered if maybe I ought to take a tip from Rachel and be happier *not knowing.* I thought about watching something more escapist. An old Don Knotts movie, maybe. *The Incredible Mr. Limpet.*

But for me, not knowing is not an option.

I waited through the snow and black screen. Then the usual feature-film FBI warning came on. This startled me. But I told myself it was OK, Vlad must have just recorded over a film.

Then the film started. And it did feature O.J. Simpson. It was the cheesy '70s disaster picture *The Towering Inferno.*

"What the fuck?" I said.

I did a fast-forward, looking for where the murder footage began. But it never came. I went through the whole tape, only stopping to watch at real speed the lame sequence where Simpson, as a fireman, rescues a group of people from the burning skyscraper. He was young and pretty with a moderate Afro. I'd forgotten how *pretty* he once was, how shiny and, well, *juicy* and kissy-faced.

I picked up the phone.

I got Vlad's service and left this message: "Look, I don't know what your game is, but I'm not playing it. You gave me *The Towering Inferno.* If it was an honest mistake, or whatever, you'd fucking well better call me back. Pronto. Asshole."

He didn't call back.

The next day I tried to reach Vlad at the Russian Consulate, but I was told he'd called in sick. I drove down to his house—with my eye on the rearview mirror. But there was no sign of anyone following me.

I rang the bell several times and knocked but got no answer. I walked around to his driveway to check for his car. And that's when his neighbor, an old lady with a Hispanic accent working in her rose garden, said, "He go. He take his clothes. Very fast."

"When?"

"Maybe 3, 4."

"In the morning?"

"*Si.* He wake me up. He throw his clothes in the car. Other things. Like he no come back."

"That's odd."

"He look scared. You his friend?"

"Yes," I told her. "We're very close. This is quite disturbing. I think I'm going to check things out a bit, if you'll excuse me."

I cut around to the backyard, where I jimmied open a sliding glass door. Which is *not* hard to do.

His neighbor was right. His closet was half empty. So were most of the bedroom drawers. Clothes scattered. He'd left in a hurry.

I was careful as I checked around, using a dish towel when I touched anything so I wouldn't leave prints. Just in case of...whatever. And then I remembered I'd been in there just the night before and left prints all over. In his messy home office, I turned on his computer. A nice looking setup, but there was nothing on it, not even an operating system. It could have been messed up for a while for all I knew. But I suspected that before he took off he'd erased the hard drive.

I looked through his desk drawers, and that's where I hit pay dirt. In the bottom drawer, in an envelope filled with travel photos—heavyset Russians at the Grand Canyon, Yellowstone, Carlsbad Caverns—I found a brief note to Vlad written in bad English and a feminine hand. With a Costa Mesa return address. I guessed the note was probably from his sister-in-law, the one in Orange County he'd visited the day of the murder.

As I was leaving, the neighbor asked, "What you find?"

"Not much," I said. "I may call his wife's sister."

She shook her head. "It's sad."

I almost let it go, but said, "What do you mean?"

"His wife. The way she die. I hear the shot."

"His wife was shot?"

She stopped her pruning, looking puzzled. "You say you are his friend?"

"I am. I'm a very old friend. From Chicago. We haven't actually spoken for some time."

She sighed. "Then you don't know. His wife shoot herself. Here." She pointed to her mouth. "Is strange, no? Men use the gun. Women take pills. I never hear of a woman who use a gun before."

"Neither have I," I said, in cold shock. "I...I can't believe it. *Why?*"

"This I do not know. But they both drink, you know. They drink and fight. I hear it. But to do such a thing in front of him is horrible! The police arrive and the ambulance. But it is too late. He is sobbing right here in the yard. 'Why? Why? Why?' Very painful."

I looked across the street at the former Nicole Simpson condo. "This block has bad karma."

"Karma? I do not know this word."

"It's not important," I said. "When did this happen?"

"One week ago last night."

"I see. Thank you for telling me. I am definitely going to find Vlad. It sounds as if he's suffering."

I was heading for my car when she said, "You tell him I give his wife's tape to her sister."

I wheeled around. "Tape?"

"The wedding tape."

"Wedding tape?"

"His wife come to my door one night. Two weeks ago. They are fighting and she say, 'Please keep this for me. He was going to destroy it.'"

"And she said it was their *wedding tape*?"

She nodded. "Yes. He was quite drunk. And you know how drunk men get. So I kept it for her."

"I take it you didn't watch it."

"It did not interest me."

"When did you give it to her sister?"

"On the night his wife die. I give it to her because he was too crazy with grief."

"I see. Her sister in Costa Mesa?"

She shrugged. "I don't know where she lives."

"Well, thank you. You've been very helpful."

"I hope he's all right."

I drove off. And stopped a few blocks away to study my Thomas Guide map of Southern California, to locate the Costa Mesa address. I found it on the map. It was shortly after 10 o'clock. I got on the 405 freeway, heading south.

I reached the house around 11:30. Actually, I drove right past it, having spotted a black Lexus with diplomatic plates parked in front. I parked around the corner and made my way back to the house on foot.

It was a cheap '50s tract house, typical of Costa Mesa. Bedraggled palm bushes, concrete pagodas in the flower beds, white rock roof. I sneaked alongside the house to where I could peek in through a den window. That's where I saw Vlad and four other Russians, speaking in their native tongue as they watched the Simpson murder tape on a crummy TV.

The tape was nearly over. I'd missed the action, as it were. O.J.—or someone or some*thing* that looked exactly like him—stood over Nicole's corpse with a knife in his hand. He was winded, as you might expect. He glanced around, and, once again, as in the still photo, I saw the crazed glint in his eyes. Then he wiped the knife on his dark warm-up suit and, as alleged in the trials, took off at a brisk pace down the walkway toward the Bundy Drive back alley. Once he disappeared from view, the tape cut to snow.

The other Russians, all in their 40s and casually attired, appeared stunned. Clearly they hadn't seen the tape before. Vlad, on the other hand, was somewhat cocky as he removed the cassette from the VCR. More words were exchanged in Russian. Then everybody got up. I ducked as one of the men absently glanced at the window, as if he intuited they were being watched. But he missed me.

Still, I was afraid to look in again, afraid they might spot me. So I was still crouching behind some palm bushes, getting a sense from the tone of their conversation that they might all be about to leave, when I heard someone step into the next room, which I could tell from the height of the small window was a bathroom.

I sneaked over to that window and peered in. Vlad taking a leak while humming "Moscow Nights."

Then I saw the videocassette resting on the counter by the sink. The window was open and there was no screen. Vlad had his back to me as he pissed. I gauged that if I leaned in, I might be able to reach the cassette. And so I tried.

The first time I failed. I could touch the counter, but the cassette was a maddening few inches from my fingertips. I tried again, on tiptoes. And this time I got it. With my fingertips I pulled the cassette across the countertop until I could grab it.

I nearly got away clean.

But before I could step away from the window, Vlad shook off, zipped up, turned, and saw me.

A few seconds more and he never would've known it was me.

"Hey!"

I dashed through the backyard, thinking about the best way to get back to my car, assuming they'd think I'd parked out front. I knew there was an alley, so I headed for that.

I had to pass a small swimming pool in the backyard—where I would've stopped in shock if I hadn't known they were coming after me. In the pool was the body of a woman floating facedown. Except she didn't have a face. More to the point, she didn't have a head. What she had was a lot of pink water around her and a fat, pale body that was 30 years too old for its turquoise thong bikini.

I kept running, hitting the alley full-stride. After a few seconds I realized they weren't on my tail. They'd gone out the front, believing I had too. Which doesn't mean I *walked* to my car. But the getaway was clean.

I headed back to Rachel's, driving an indirect route and doubling back a couple of times to make sure Vlad and his gang weren't following. Vlad's sister must have had the tape and not wanted to cough it up. Maybe thinking, as I had, that it was worth a lot more than 65 grand.

All the way back I kept wondering what they'd done with her head.

Rachel was still at work, so I stuck the cassette in the VCR.

It went like this.

At the point where the tape began, Nicole and O.J. were standing, just the two of them, in the open Bundy gate. They were talking. He was agitated, clearly. He was angry, and Nicole was trying to cool him down. You couldn't hear their words, but those were the tones of their voices.

Then, without warning, O.J. pulled out a short knife. And now his words were clear: "You fucking bitch. You fucked with my head for the last time."

I gasped as O.J. stabbed Nicole.

As with the still photos, the tape was not razor sharp, but there was no doubt as to who the people were. They were not look-alikes. It was not staged. It was them. It was real.

O.J. had stabbed Nicole several times when a second man abruptly stepped into the frame, yelling, "Hey, hey, hey!" This was Ron Goldman. When he tried to pull O.J. away from Nicole, the ex-football star turned on him.

Well, you know the rest. There's no need for yet another retelling or even a blow-by-blow. It's enough to say that the first trial description of Goldman being trapped in the fenced area "like a caged animal" was accurate. He tried to stave off Simpson's slashes and stabs, but it was hopeless.

I nearly had to look away when he went back to finish off Nicole.

Then I went to the bathroom and dry heaved.

When that was over, I rewound the tape and watched it several more times in slow motion.

The next morning I took the tape to my friend Ken, who worked at a special effects lab in Venice Beach. He also had a state-of-the-art computer editing setup at home. He described himself in one of his AOL screen profile names as: "Film buff, great masturbator, premier technogeek." If anyone could tell me if the tape was real, it was Ken.

After he'd seen it once at real speed he said, "Wow." We were sitting in front of the largest of several monitors in his small, hardware crammed apartment overlooking the Venice Beach boardwalk. Behind his thick glasses, he looked dazed. "Jesus fucking shit!"

"So what do you think?" I said. "Is it real?"

"First impression? Gut impression?"

I nodded.

Ken shut off the VCR and took a deep breath of ocean air. "I think it's real," he said. "That's my impression. If it's not...it's a work of incredible skill."

"Nothing struck you as fake right off the bat?"

"I just told you, Jim. I think it's probably real."

"I need to know for sure. There can't be any doubt."

He leaned back in his chartreuse velour armchair. He had on plaid polyester pants and an ugly sky blue disco-era body shirt that showed off his potbelly. I think this was all intentionally kitsch, since he was a serious Beck fan. But I'm not sure. "Well," he said. "To know for sure will take some time."

"Can't you just study the pixels and—"

"Jim, there aren't any pixels. This isn't a photograph or a digitized image. It's a videotape. The only way to know is to study it frame by frame."

"If it were faked," I said, "how would someone fake it?"

"It wouldn't be easy, but it could be done. You'd get actors to play out the scene. Then you'd need different photos of all the principals. Which in this case wouldn't be hard to come by. But to make it all blend, to make it all seamless would take a lot of time and ability. Though not as much as it used to, even a few years ago. But it would take a *long* time to come up with something this good."

"What about the location?"

"Well, they wouldn't have to *go* there, if that's what you mean. They could shoot the actors against a blue screen. But then you would need separate footage of the Bundy gate from just the right angle. If they're saying it was shot from inside a neighbor's house..."

"Whoever made the tape would need access to the house."

"Right. I assume you can't tell me where you got this?"

"It's better if you don't know. Believe me."

"I understand."

"How long will it take for you to know for sure?"

Ken tapped his pencil on his desktop. "I can't really say. I'll do as much as I can tonight and tomorrow. If I haven't found anything truly egregious by the end of the day tomorrow, I can let you know *that.* But I can't really say when I'll know for sure. I'll work on it as much as I can."

I finished off the Diet Coke he'd given me. "Look, I'm really trusting you here. You know what this is. How big this is. If it's real, the whole world is going to see it very soon, I assure you. But in the meantime, you have to promise me—"

"I promise," he said. "I won't mention it to anyone. Let alone show it."

"And you have to promise not to make a dub. I know how you are, Ken."

He smiled faintly, as I knew he would. It still bothered me, though.

"I mean it, Ken."

He did have a sizable weird tape collection.

"I promise," he said. "I won't make a dub. This is too serious. It's not like a tape of Chuck Berry pissing on some woman with a blond bouffant in a bathtub."

This was one of the oddball tapes in his collection, which also looked real. Although the tape, a film originally, had been through so many generations that while you could still make out a fuzzy, faded Chuck, the main thing identifying the singer was his voice.

"OK." I got up. "Can you hide it in someplace safe when you're not working on it? I mean, outside of this apartment."

"Why?" For the first time, I caught some fear from him. "You said no one knew you were bringing it here."

"No one does know. But there are people looking for this."

"What aren't you telling me?"

"Nothing in particular," I said, omitting Linkletter, Vlad, the headless body, and my Morrissey impersonation. "I'm just a tad paranoid, that's all. Since this is the only copy I have. And as far as I know, there aren't any others. And if it's real, it does prove he did it. So..."

"I have a place I can hide it," he said. "A place I sometimes hide my drugs. OK?"

"I'd feel better."

Not much later, I left. And I wasn't that worried. I'd been careful and watchful driving over. And I did trust Ken. That is, I knew I could trust him not to call the cops, not to call the media, and not to sell it. But I did know Ken. The matter of the dub was what bothered me. I wondered if he might find that prospect irresistible. Just to have it for his collection. The upside on that: Ken was basically a wuss and not a good liar. Whenever I came to get the tape back, I planned to pin him to the wall, figuratively, on the dub thing. If he'd made one, I was pretty sure I could get it out of him.

That night I watched television with Rachel. The murder in Costa Mesa made the evening national news. We watched the Tom Brokaw version. The story might have remained local except for the way it broke: Vlad's mother-in-law had opened a FedEx box in Moscow that contained the severed head of her daughter.

Rachel and I assumed she screamed.

They'd traced the head back to the body, which was still floating in her Costa Mesa pool. The motive for the murder wasn't yet known. But Vlad, who'd disappeared, was mentioned by name as a suspect, and as a "low-level diplomat with the Los Angeles consulate, rumored to have Russian Mafia ties."

"A Russian Mafia tie?" Rachel said. "Is that anything like a Jerry Garcia tie?"

"Yeah. They've got little pictures of Boris Yeltsin dancing. Until, near the bottom of the tie, where he starts to have a heart attack."

Rachel and I share a dark sense of humor.

Still, the whole matter was creeping me out since I'd seen it firsthand. And now I had the Russian Mafia looking for me.

"Oh," said Rachel, midway through the news. "Some guy named Linkletter called."

"Art?"

"No. But that's the only first name I can think of that fits with Linkletter. He sounded angry, and he wants you to call him."

"Thanks."

I wasn't half as worried about Linkletter as I was about Vlad. I mean, what kind of sick bastard cuts off his wife's sister's head and mails it to her mother?

The next morning I phoned Ken to see if he'd come up with anything.

"It's like I told you," he said. "I'm looking at it frame by frame. That's the only way to know."

"And?"

"I'm still looking at it, Jim." He sounded irritated.

"How far are you into it?"

"He's still stabbing Nicole."

"But it looks real so far?"

"Yeah. I've been paying special attention to the faces. The facial expressions. If it *is* a simulation...well, it's beyond very good. But the technology has improved so much that almost anything is possible now."

"When do you think you'll be able to make a final call?"

"Still can't say. It gets trickier once he goes after Goldman. Much more complex."

"Ballpark figure."

"Give me through the end of the day. Of course, if I spot something that blows it, I'll call you right away."

It all sounded good. But I had a funny feeling that Ken might be up to something. That he might be stalling me. So I decided to pay him a visit.

On the way to Venice Beach I phoned Linkletter.

As soon as he realized it was me, he said, "OK. Where's the tape? And spare me the shit. I know you've got it."

"Well, I did talk to Vlad—"

"I said, spare me the shit. You were in Costa Mesa. A neighbor gave a description. You snagged the tape through the bathroom window."

"A neighbor saw me do *that*?"

"Where's the damn tape?"

"It's being examined," I said. "To see if it's real. That's all I'm going to tell you."

"Look," he said, "you *could* be in deep shit. So far I haven't told the feds it was you in Costa Mesa. But that could change if I don't get that tape."

"If you fuck with me, you'll never see the tape. And neither will whoever it is that put up the hundred grand."

"You're way out of your league."

"I'll call you in a couple of days."

"You're an asshole."

I hung up.

"Who is it?" Ken said when I knocked on his door.

"It's Jim. Open up."

"Hold on a second." His voice was shaky.

"Now!"

He undid the deadbolt and opened the door. As soon as I saw his face, I knew he was up to something. He had a nervous, furtive air, almost laughably reeking of guilt.

I noted the murder scene playing on his monitor, and a VCR and a DVD running side by side.

"You fucking weasel. You're making a dub."

"No. I'm not. I'm just—"

"Ken, goddamn you." I checked the VCR and DVD connections. He *was* making a dub. "You sneaky piece of shit." I shut off the DVD, ejected the disk. "I trusted you." I stopped the VCR and ejected the tape, the original.

He caved. "Look, I'm sorry. But I couldn't *not* make a copy. I mean, this is on par with the Zapruder film! How could I not make a copy, just for myself? I swear, that's all I was doing."

"Is this the only dub?"

"Yes. I mean, of course. I was just starting to make it."

I sensed he might be lying. Then I looked at all the videocassettes and DVDs on his worktable, in rows that filled the shelves lining his walls. It would take days to look at all of them.

"Tell me the truth, Ken."

"I am! Look, I'm sorry. But you know me, Jim. You must have known I couldn't resist."

"So did you make a decision?"

"A decision?"

"Is it real? Is the tape real?"

"Oh. Yes. It is."

"Are you sure?"

"I went through it frame by frame. Some parts several times. The stuff with Goldman—that's what sold me. That was too complex to fake. The facial expressions. When they change, if it were fake, there'd be glitches. Stuff you wouldn't catch at normal speed, but frame by frame you would. I'm certain it's real."

"Completely certain?"

"I'd stake my life on it."

"Thank you," I said. "I appreciate your help." Then I left with both the original tape and the dub he'd been making.

When I got back to Rachel's I watched the original again. Once, twice. After the second viewing I almost picked up the phone. To call a legal reporter at a local TV station, a guy I was friendly with, who'd covered the Simpson case. I knew he'd come in his pants when I told him what I had. My hand was on the phone, but I hesitated.

And then...I watched the tape again. I'd seen it enough times by now that I was detached. The initial horror factor had dissipated. I slow-motioned through the Goldman killing. And I saw what Ken meant, even though I wasn't an expert. The facial expressions were smooth and convincing.

Still, something about the tape bothered me. It *looked* flawless, but it *felt* flawed. I decided to trust my instincts and sit on the tape, at least for another day.

I also decided that Rachel's wasn't a good place for me to be staying. It was cozy but not very secure. I called my friend Phil, a director who I knew was shooting on location in Spain. I'd stayed at his place in the Palisades a couple of times, and it was practically a vault. In fact, that's what he'd named it: the Vault.

Phil told me that the security code hadn't changed since I'd last stayed there, and to make myself at home.

I left Rachel a nice note and headed to Phil's place. It was less a house than a fortress, a post-Frank Gehry citadel of rough, reinforced concrete, built to stave off burglars, brush fires, and dystopian terrorists. Set in the hills beyond Amalfi Drive, it overlooked the emerald golf course of the Riviera Country Club, where the Juice used to play before the members barred him. From the lushly gardened second-floor terrace you could also see the ocean, as well as the Palos Verde peninsula. The building's interior was warm and comfortable, filled with overstuffed chairs and sofas and expensive art and country antiques. But it was still like a vault—a homey vault, with an electronic gate, security cameras, and blast-proof steel doors. There were no ground floor windows, no windows anywhere that would allow a sharpshooter to get you in his sights.

I decided to unwind with a long, hot shower. And it was there, surrounded by white marble with the water pounding on me and steam billowing in thick clouds, that it suddenly hit me. I quickly dried off, pulled on a pair of boxers, and watched the tape yet again, this time on one of Phil's many VCRs. I watched it almost all the way through—right up to where O.J., having finally killed Ron Goldman, returns to Nicole to finish her off. I watched him crouch down behind her and pull her head back by her hair. I watched him slit her throat with the knife. I used the remote several times to replay that action, because *that* was where the problem was.

I stopped the tape and called my journalist friend at his home in Manhattan Beach.

When he heard my voice on his machine he picked up.

"I have a question about the Simpson case," I said.

"Shoot."

"OK, it's this. When the killer slit Nicole's throat, how did he hold the knife? I mean, did he hold it with the blade sticking out between his thumb and forefinger, or the other way, with the blade sticking out from the lower part of his hand—the way you'd hold it if you were stabbing someone with a hammer-like motion?"

"That's an interesting question," he said, "because it was initially assumed that the killer did it the first way. The way you'd normally see someone slit a throat. In a film, for example. From behind the victim. But the knife used, contrary to popular belief, was not that large, nor was it razor sharp. And, as you know, he cut her throat so deeply that the blade nicked her spinal column. He nearly decapitated her."

"Yes, I know."

"So, to answer your question, the coroner determined that he'd held the knife with the blade sticking out from the *lower* part of the hand—in a hammer-like position, as you describe it. Holding the knife in that manner, he stabbed her in the neck and drew the knife across her throat. That's what gave him the leverage to cut as deeply as he did."

"Are you sure about this?" I asked. "I mean, the coroner wasn't what you'd call—"

"Yes, I know. In fact, the original coroner did make the wrong assumption. But a subsequent study of the wounds and the autopsy photos by a number of other, much more competent individuals reached the conclusion I've just given you. So yes, I'd say at this point there's no doubt." Then, inevitably, he added, "Why do you ask?"

"Just something I'm working on," I said. "Experimental fiction. Can't go into it. You know how I am about works in progress. But I needed to get this right. I can't thank you enough."

Once I got off the phone, I ran the tape again, just to affirm what I already knew.

In the tape, "Simpson" slit "Nicole's" throat the customary way, holding the knife so the blade jutted out from between his thumb and forefinger. *As opposed to the way it actually happened.*

That was why the tape had seemed flawed. And that was why, no matter how real it looked, no matter how impervious to detection it seemed to be, the tape was a fake. A *perfect* fake. That is, perfect in and of itself. But fatally flawed as an accurate record.

But, then again, the issue had been contended. What if the tape was right and the experts wrong? In court, which holds up better as evidence: a tape that has passed every simulation test or the *interpretation* of a group of pathologists?

At exactly this point in my thinking, my cell phone rang.

It was Vlad. He said, "Hey fuck. You dirty fuck."

"Vlad! My word, it's *you*!" I went into my vaguely British, cheerfully fey shtick. "How *are* you, cupcake? I've been concerned about you. Did you know you're wanted? Have been ever since you chopped off sissy's noggin, you naughty boy, you."

"Listen, you rotten fuck. You think that was bad, wait until you see what we do to your mother."

"Vlad, lovey, that's sick. And silly. My mother was killed in a car crash years ago." This wasn't true, by the way. But since becoming "controversial," I've made sure my mother is very difficult to locate.

"So we'll dig her up and send you the head. How would you like that, you filthy fuck?"

"Well, I wouldn't," I said, still cheerfully fey. "That should go without saying. But you're still not getting your tape back, you psychotic stool sample."

"You think you're so smart," he said. "But we are going to find you."

I didn't think it was too smart of him to let me know they were clueless as to my whereabouts. "Vlad, dear," I said, "as long as we're talking, you might like to know that your sister-in-law lost her head over nothing. The tape's a fraud, angel, in case you don't already know. But then, of course, you must know, mustn't you?"

"You're full of shit. I tell you the truth. I shoot that myself the night of the killings."

"Well, I don't really care to go into detail, but I have strong reason to disbelieve you." I wasn't about to tell him where whoever had made the tape had fucked up so they could rectify the error.

"I don't care what you think," he said. "We are hot on your trail, fuckface. I call you back when I have a hostage, huh? Your mother might be dead, but you still got friends, no?"

With that, he hung up.

I thought about Rachel. I knew her mother in upstate New York would not enjoy receiving *her* head in a box.

I was sitting on the sofa trying to think of a way to caution Rachel without scaring the shit out of her, when my phone rang again. I assumed it was Vlad. "What now?" I said.

"Hello?"

Not Vlad. This was a woman.

"I'd like to speak with James Robert Baker, please."

With her husky voice she sounded like...Diane Rainey.

"This is Diane Rainey," she said.

I'd never met Diane, but what I knew of her I didn't like, and I never cared for her work, and her husband was a right-wing cretin. But it never hurts to be cordial to big stars. "This is James," I said. "What can I do for you?" Because, let's face it, Diane Rainey was a *very* big star.

"Well, James," she said, "I think I have a situation that may be of great benefit to us both."

"If you're talking about a script situation or a rewrite or something, you should really have your people discuss it with my people and then—"

"It's not a script," she said. "Is this phone secure?"

"It's my cell phone. Look, if this is some kind of phone sex thing, you've got the wrong guy. In more ways than one."

"I was warned you'd be flip," she said. "I expected that. So let me cut to the chase. I have a problem. A *serious* problem. And I think you can help me solve it. If you can, you're welcome to the proceeds of the solution. Which, trust me, will far exceed your wildest dreams."

"That's a little vague," I said.

"I don't think it's wise to tell you anything more over the telephone. You'll understand why when I do tell you. Can you come to my house? I'm in the Palisades."

At least she was nearby.

If I were Philip Marlowe, I'd say it was one of those fake Santa Fe jobs they threw up in the 1980s. There was a lot of architectural throwing up in the '80s, if you remember. And this piece of ersatz adobe vomit was splattered across a few acres at the end of San Remo Drive, less than a mile from the Vault. San Remo was the street Ron and Nancy had lived on before moving to the White House. I passed the address on my way to Diane's and was relieved to see that the ugly old Gipper bunker had finally been torn down to make way for a mammoth new lot filler.

Diane buzzed me through her gate, and I parked in the courtyard beside her Bentley. I'd driven Phil's Range Rover, not wanting to risk driving my recognizable light blue 1968 Citroën.

She met me at the door. That's when I reeled. At first I

thought she'd sent an assistant. An extremely obese assistant. *Extremely* obese. But then I saw her face, and I couldn't stop myself from saying, *"Jesus!"*

"I know," she said, and there were tears in her eyes. "I'm supposed to be pregnant, taking some time off. That's the cover story." She checked me out nervously. "You don't have a camera, do you?"

"My God," I said. "What happened?"

I mean, here was a woman who'd based her career in large part on her Hollywood-toned body.

"Come in," she said, "and I'll tell you."

She led me into a den filled with Spanish-style furniture.

"I'll be honest." She collapsed onto a couch. "I was taking steroids and a fistful of other weight-control drugs, some Chinese herbs and other dicey items, including a rare Tibetan fungus. They all worked wonderfully for a long time. In fact, I barely had to exercise, the mixture worked so well. Then, suddenly last summer my body rebelled and went biochemically berserk. A kind of rebound effect. No matter how little I eat now, or what I eat, I keep piling on pounds. I've tried fasting. I've tried bulimia. I even did liposuction. But nothing works. Nothing stops it. By the time the bruises healed from the lipo, I'd gained the weight back. My body has become a blubber machine."

"Jesus," I said. "I'm sorry." And I was. I mean, I felt bad for her, just on a human level. Even though I still thought she was a dimwit married to a scumbag. So my sympathy had a cap.

"I've tried everything," she said. "I've seen all the doctors. They all tell me what I just told you. It's my own fault. It's a kind of karmic payback. Maybe God didn't want me to get

10 million just for showing my tits in *Final Obsession.*"

At the time, that had been a record. But then Demi Moore got 12 million for *Striptease.*

"Maybe God's trying to tell me my tits aren't worth that much. When there are still so many little children starving."

She looked sad, thinking of all the little starving children.

"You may be right," I said. "God's an odd bird."

"I've tried to set things right," she said. "I've given money to Feed the Children. I've even given money to AIDS research. Biff nearly shit when I did that." Biff Decker: her homophobic star hubby. "I've given hundreds of thousands. *But I'm still getting fat!*"

Diane began to sob outright. It was awkward. I felt I should do something. Put my arm around her or something like that. But I was sitting a good 10 feet away, and I couldn't motivate myself to get up and cross the room.

Finally a short Latina maid floated into the room with club sodas for both of us and a box of Kleenex for Diane. I thanked the maid, but Diane ignored her. Diane blew her nose and blotted her eyes. I took a sip of the iced and limed club soda.

"I understand your plight," I said. "What I don't understand is why you think I can help."

"Because," she said, "you live on the edge. You don't just observe and then sit at a computer and write. You get out and live. And then you write about that. Like...what's his name?"

"Dostoyevsky?"

"No. *Fear and Loathing.*"

"Søren Kierkegaard?"

"No, no. You know, that crazy leftist with the guns and drugs."

"Ah, Hunter Thompson. He prefers that we not speak of it,

but we were fuck buddies at the 1968 Democratic Convention. Tear gas and stolen kisses."

She looked confused. "I don't know what you mean by that, and I don't think I care to. I'll be honest: I don't think I like you. I don't care for your politics or your perverted lifestyle. But I do admire the way you handled that awful *Sea Crew* situation. Yes, I heard about that. And I'm compelled to admit you've got balls."

"Thanks. I don't think I like you either."

"You don't have to be rude."

"Fuck you," I said.

She tightened—emotionally if not physically, the latter being impossible, as she sat squashed into the sofa like a silk-covered Holstein. "Maybe this wasn't such a good idea," she said. "Maybe you're not the right man for the job after all."

I got up to leave.

But Diane couldn't get up, not without help. Which, in retrospect, I think may have been a crucial factor in why she changed course.

"All right," she said. "*Cut!* Let's start this scene over. Take it from the top. With new dialogue."

I stopped and looked back at her. "Your line."

"I need you to find a miracle diet pill."

"Miracle diet pill?" I nearly laughed.

"If you can find it for me, if it really works, it will be yours to do with as you please. And, of course, if it works, it *will* be worth a fortune."

"I'm sure," I said, still trying not to laugh.

"I can see you don't believe me," she said. "I'm telling you this is real. I heard about it from another writer, a British historian that I hired as a technical adviser when we were making *The Night England Wept."* Her early-'90s World War II romance stinker. "The pill has a name. It's sometimes referred to as the Berchtesgaden Diet."

With this, she snagged my full attention. I *had* heard of this. Eva Braun's method for staying slim and pert for her man. As I recalled, Eva shared Hitler's vegetarianism, which would have cut the blood sausage and weisswurst from her diet. And there were rumors that the Führer's personal physician had also helped with pills and injections—a special preparation that kept the weight off, the formula to which was lost in the final days of the war.

"According to the British historian—"

"Trevor Leland?" I said.

"You know him?"

"We're old enemies." My feud with Trevor went back to a *New York Times* review I'd written of his crackpot pseudohistory *Inside Hitler's Brain*, in which he "proved" that Hitler was gay. I'd shredded him, and he hadn't taken it well. After several nasty back-and-forth letters to the editor, he'd tried to sue me for libel and defamation. Eventually the case was thrown out, but not before I'd spent thousands on legal fees.

"Well," said Diane, "according to Trevor, Eva Braun had a special pill she took. And I know what you're thinking, but it wasn't just amphetamine. It may have contained *some* amphetamine, and perhaps some B-12. But there was another secret and critical ingredient."

"Trevor told you this?"

"Yes. Of course at the time I didn't care all that much. I was curious, of course, but I was on my own regimen, which was working so well... The principle involved with Eva's little pill is alleged to be 'the more you eat, the more you lose.'"

"I don't see how that would be possible."

"I don't either. But supposedly it is. According to Trevor, Eva had a weakness for sticky pastries. At night she would sneak down to the Berghof kitchen and, well, I suppose the only term is 'pig out.' Entire chocolate layer cakes, gooey Napoleons, strudel. And the more she ate, the more weight she lost. Exactly the opposite of what's happening to me."

"Have you talked with Trevor recently?"

"I got back in touch with him after the liposuction failed. He says he knows more now than when I met him on location with *England Wept.* He's found someone who knows the location of the last remaining pills. Someone who was a part of Hitler's inner circle, who is very old now and likely to die soon. But this person refuses to talk unless Trevor pays a huge sum of money. Which he's reluctant to do, since it could be a scam."

"So where do I figure in?"

"Can I be blunt?"

"You have been so far."

"Trevor's a gentleman. You're not."

"Meaning? Not that I can't guess."

"He's too polite. I believe the person who claims to know where the pills are may be a woman. Old. No doubt quite frail. Possibly one of Hitler's former secretaries."

"And...?"

"Trevor doesn't have what it takes to lean on this person, if you get my drift. I thought that might be less of a problem for you."

"You thought I wouldn't mind beating the truth out of some old Nazi bitch."

"In a word, yes." She paused. "*Would* you mind?"

"Not on principle."

"If you can do this," she said, "if you can bring me these pills, I have a doctor who's willing to analyze the contents and manufacture doses for me. And I'll pay you $500,000. Half up front, which should more than cover expenses. The rest on delivery. Plus, except for my personal supply, you'll have the formula to yourself, to do with as you please. If the pills work, that could mean *millions. Billions,* even. So what do you think?"

I sat silently, not sure what I thought.

She stared out the window at the dry brown chaparral hills, waiting for me to answer.

I finally said, "I think...I want to give this some thought. It's not untempting. But I have a few other things going on right now."

"How much time do you need? I want to move quickly. As you can see, I'm suffering."

She was right. She was suffering, and I could see it. "Give me a day," I told her. "And let me ask you something. Given that you dislike me so much, why are you approaching me with this?"

She gave me a hard look. "Because even though I don't like you, I trust you. I don't think you'll try to fuck me the way some people might."

"I'll take that as a backhanded compliment."

"That's how I meant it."

I was right about her not being able to get up without

help. She remained on the sofa as I said goodbye.

"I'll call sometime tomorrow," I said.

"Fine. I'll be here. I'm not going anywhere, not like this."

My cell phone rang as I climbed into Phil's Range Rover. I recognized the number as Ken's and picked up. But the voice on the other end didn't belong to Ken. It was Linkletter.

"What are you doing at Ken's?" I said.

"Why don't you come on over and see? And bring the money with you."

"Cut the crap. What's going on?"

"You'll see."

He hung up.

I stopped at the Vault long enough to pick up the satchel with the 100 grand. Then I shot down to Venice.

I'd like to say I was surprised by what I found when I got there, but I wasn't.

Nearly a dozen cop cars clogged Speedway, the narrow alley-like street behind Ken's oceanfront apartment building. Black-and-whites and unmarked detectives' cars, including Linkletter's. And a coroner's van. So I knew that what I'd feared was true even before Linkletter sauntered over and confirmed it.

"I figure Vlad beat us here by about an hour," he said. "Too bad you wouldn't tell me who your expert was. He might still be alive if we'd gotten here first."

"How do you know it was Vlad?"

"He seems to have a jones for cutting off heads. Your buddy Ken's is stuffed in his monitor."

"Stuffed in his...?"

Linkletter indicated the open door of the apartment. "You wanna take a look?"

"No, thanks."

"Probably just as well. There's more. They tortured him first. Used a live wire on his privates. Then they decapitated him."

"What'd they use? A chain saw?"

"No way. Too noisy. Electric knife is my guess. Like a Thanksgiving turkey."

"Jesus. How'd you find out about him?"

"Jimbo, we're not as dumb as you think." He glanced around furtively and mumbled, "Where's the loot?"

"In my car."

I'd switched to a rental car, knowing Linkletter could run the plates on Phil's Range Rover and find out where I was staying.

"OK," he said. "Let's mosey over."

We did that.

The other cops were all focused on the crime scene, coming and going, paying us no attention. I handed the satchel to Linkletter. He casually tossed it into his own car.

"I don't suppose you found any dubs of the tape?" I asked.

"What do *you* think? The place is ripped to shit. And my guess is, if he had anything, he coughed it up before they chopped him. You ever had a live wire put to your dick?"

"No. Have you?"

Linkletter chuckled in that sick way that only cops can

chuckle. I'll be more specific: in that sick way that only *L.A.* cops can chuckle.

"Is that a yes or a no? What are you into, Frank? Sexually, I mean. Not that I really give a shit, but it's crossed my mind from time to time."

"You might be surprised," he said.

"I might be appalled. By the way, the tape's a fake."

This threw him.

"You heard me. It's perfect, technically. But they flubbed a detail. The way Nicole's throat was slit. You can even see it in the still you showed me. Check the autopsy report, and then compare."

Linkletter looked shaken. He finally said, "I'll have to check that out."

"You do that. I'm going to leave now. Ken was an old friend of mine. This is upsetting."

"I still want the original, Jim."

"It was with Ken."

"Bullshit. You already fucked up on that. You asked if we'd found a dub. If you didn't already have the original, you'd have asked about *that.*"

"I didn't ask about the original because I assumed Vlad took it. I asked about a dub because I know Ken. And the odds are good he made a dub. Have you checked his collection? It could be labeled as anything. *The Wild Bunch. Lolita. Straitjacket.*"

"We're aware of that. Every tape and disc will be checked."

"Fine. I'm leaving now," I said again. "I don't have the tape. I wish I'd never gotten involved in this. Three people are dead over this."

"Three? I only count two."

"Vlad's wife. I'm pretty sure he killed her."

"Oh, right. The suicide. I want that tape, Jimbo."

"Diane?"

"Jim?"

"We're on."

Trevor's house was within walking distance of my London hotel. It was a stately Georgian place on a helplessly pleasant stretch of Cheyne Walk, overlooking the Thames. I arrived around 10 in the morning, stepping through an unlocked iron gate. I climbed the steps and rang the doorbell, aware that Trevor would be watching via the overhead surveillance camera.

I was betting he'd be alone. And paranoid. A British tabloid had excerpted from a forthcoming book in which Trevor contended, this time, that Hitler knew nothing of the Holocaust until his last days in the bunker. It was all Himmler's doing, according to Trevor. And in a truly vile scene, Trevor depicted Hitler's "shock" in the Berlin bunker as a Wehrmacht officer finally told him what his SS chief had been up to. To quote: *"Mein Gott!"* Hitler exclaimed, the blood draining from his weary face. "They are killing the Jews at Auschwitz? Himmler is doing this? How can it be? This is unbelievable! How could he do such a thing on his own? As much as I dislike certain aspects of the Jews, I would never have approved of such a thing as this!"

This is an indication of what a true scumbag Diane Rainey was, in that she would hire this lunatic as a film's technical adviser.

I rang Trevor's bell a second time before I heard his shaky voice over the intercom. "I can see who you are," he said. "And I'm calling the authorities right now."

"Trevor, wait," I said calmly. "I'm not here to harm you."

"Who are you working for? The Israelis or the American Jews?"

"I'm not working for anyone." I held up a manuscript folder I'd brought along. "Odd as it may seem, I've come to help you. To help both of us, actually. I was doing my own research for a novel about Hitler's last days, and... Could you let me in? I'm sure you know I'm unarmed. Your gate contains a metal detector. Trevor, I don't like yelling this out on the street."

"You needn't yell," he said through the intercom. "I can hear you quite well. Please go on."

I held up the folder. "I can't tell you how, but I came into possession of the final letters written in the bunker by Eva Braun. And they prove beyond all doubt that you're right about Hitler's lack of knowledge of the Holocaust. She writes about his shock—"

"His what?"

"His shock. And hers too. And how upset he was because he knew what it would do to his reputation."

"His reputation, yes..."

Trevor sounded older than he was, which was maybe 60.

He also sounded a little senile, or at least befuddled. And he was beginning to buy my line.

"He was *not* an evil monster!" I yelled into the intercom as I waved the folder. "And these letters *prove* it!"

I heard the longed-for buzz.

I pushed open the black door.

Entering the dim foyer, I heard him call: "I'm back here. In the solarium."

I made my way through the house, which was filled with heavy, ugly Victorian furniture and smelled of moldy cheese. I kept an eye out for servants or secretaries but saw no one.

Then we were face to face in the solarium, a dirty room filled with straggly plants, overlooking a neglected garden. Trevor did not look good. His hair, what there was of it, was white and wispy, and his skin had a yellow tinge, as if his liver might be going bad. And he sat in a chrome wheelchair, a soiled blanket over his legs.

I smiled. I'd forgotten he'd been in a car accident that had left him paralyzed from the waist down. This was going to be much easier than I'd hoped. I almost felt sorry for him.

He recognized his error immediately. "This is a trick. Isn't it? You've come here to kill me." He reached for the phone. "I'm calling the police."

I knocked his hand away and tore the phone cord from the wall.

Standing over him, I cut loose: "Listen to me, you pus-brained Nazi-loving slime. I want some information. About Eva Braun's secret diet pill."

"What? What are you talking about?"

"Don't play dumb. Someone in Hitler's inner circle told you about Eva's pills. *Who was it?*"

"I don't remember."

"If you don't tell me," I said quietly, "I'm going to knock over your wheelchair. Then I'm going to make you crawl across the floor, to where I'm going to take a piss. Then I'm going to make you lick up my urine. Understand? I'm going to make you lick my piss off this filthy floor. If you don't tell me what I want to know, that's only the beginning."

He was trembling now, his eyes bugging. I was reminded of the writer in *A Clockwork Orange,* a similar shot of *his* eyes bugging after Alec taped a rubber ball in his mouth.

"I'm trying," Trevor said. "I'm trying to remember. My mind is not... I've been on drugs since the accident. Percocet. Demerol. For the pain. I'm addicted."

"Someone in the inner circle," I prompted. "Someone still alive. That can only be a handful of people." I took a guess. "Is Trudl Junge still alive?" Hitler's chief secretary in the bunker.

"It wasn't Trudl," he said. "It was—" Unbelievably, he suddenly clutched his chest, as if he were having a heart attack.

This, I wasn't buying. Until he said, "On the table. My pills."

Amid a cluster of pill bottles on the table beside him, I found the nitroglycerin tablets, opened the bottle, and stuck one under his tongue.

Then I waited for several long minutes to see what would happen. It would have seemed too inane, not to say tritely melodramatic, if he were to croak on the verge of giving a name.

At last, still taking deep breaths, he began to calm down. "There. It's all right. Just angina. Not as bad as it looks."

"Fine. Good to hear it. You were about to say...?"

"Heidi," he said. "Heidi Schultz. The assistant secretary."

I'd read of her.

"At the very end she was still only 19," he said.

"And Eva gave her some of these pills?"

"I believe this is true. It was the night before the end of the war. Before the end in the bunker. After the wedding party."

"And...?"

"And Eva drew Heidi aside and said, 'I want you to have these.' Heidi was plump, you see. Or perhaps more than plump. Eva had taken a liking to her and wanted to help. So she gave Heidi some of the pills. She said, 'Use these pills wisely. They will help you lose weight, my dear, and they are your key to enormous financial success after the war.'"

"So why didn't Heidi cash in?"

"Because she lost the pills during her escape from Berlin. She was part of the group that fled the bunker at the last possible moment, as the Red Army was closing in from all sides. She was literally ducking bomb blasts. It was chaos, as you can imagine. But..."

"Yes?"

"She thinks the pills have almost certainly survived. But they are inaccessible to her. And only for a large sum of money will she tell me their probable location. Naturally, on the basis of such a dubious contention, I was unwilling to pay such a sum."

"Do you have any idea where the pills might be?"

"None, really, though I do know she was part of the group that reached Berchtesgaden before the German surrender. Of course the Berghof, Hitler's chief residence there, was leveled shortly after the war. *Parts* of the complex, however, remain to this day. So that's a possibility."

"I see," I said. I had a sense that I'd successfully scared him into telling what he knew. "You've been helpful."

"Are you going to kill me now?" He sounded hopeful.

I started for the door.

"You know," he said, "I don't expect you to believe this, but it was an honest mistake."

"What's that?"

"My book. The one you attacked. I did have sources, you know. Of course, I see now that they used me. But I truly did believe them initially. I really believed Hitler was a homosexual."

"Great," I said.

"But this time I'm on solid ground. Hitler really didn't know about the camps. He was no saint, I'm not saying he was. But he truly did not know about the genocide."

I sighed. If not for the wheelchair, I would have worked him over. It was still tempting. Instead I told him, "You are truly a crackpot, Trevor. Here's hoping you die before you finish your new book."

He did, by the way.

That night the BBC ran a brief story on Trevor's death. Ruled a heart attack. His body had been found in the late afternoon by a friend. I was surprised to learn he'd had any friends.

Do you know how many Heidi Schultzes there are in Germany? I'll tell you. Approximately 1.3 million. I discovered this while looking for her on my laptop. In Munich alone there were 243 Heidi Schultzes. So I switched approaches, searching for articles mentioning both Heidi Schultz and Hitler. 847 hits, mostly news articles. Mostly in English. Skimming them, it wasn't hard to see why she was written about so little in Germany—she still worshiped and defended her wartime employer. "He was fun. That's what people don't know. Hitler was fun to be with. He had *such* a sense of humor."

A 1995 British interview confirmed a Munich suburb location, "not far from the home of controversial German filmmaker Leni Riefenstahl," so I could have followed that clue and done a search on Riefenstahl. But the next Heidi article made that unnecessary. "Hitler's former secretary, now in her 70s, currently resides in a quaint cottage in the picturesque town of Berchtesgaden, the famous site of the German dictator's retreat in his beloved Bavarian Alps. They are beloved to Heidi Schultz too." This from a conservative American women's magazine, dated December 2000.

This story was by far the creepiest. "I never married, I suppose, because of my love for Hitler," Heidi confessed. "Once you've been around a man such as him, with his great magnetism, other men pale in comparison. Who could follow in his footsteps? I have yet to meet the man."

I made reservations for a flight to Munich. From there I'd have to proceed by rail to the mountain retreat.

On the last leg of the train trip to Berchtesgaden, I listened to my portable CD player, mostly to drown out the shrieks of some hyperactive *kinder* in my car. Wagner would have been more fitting than R.E.M.'s *Monster.* Or would it? Wagner might have been too facile, really. And I hate to put down a pretty landscape, but the alpine panorama was seriously kitsch. Or, more to the point, the Nazi connotation has permanently kitschified its beauty, which was stark and stupendous—the blue mountains, mists and clouds slicing their peaks, the brilliant green meadows below. But it looked like a bad painting, like Nazi art. It looked like the picture-window view from the Berghof, which is essentially what it was.

I got off the train at the Berchtesgaden station, along with the family who had the shrieking kids. But they disappeared into the hotel across the street, and I was left to ponder my next move in a sudden eerie silence.

The station was deserted. And the town, which was smaller than I'd expected, was considerably less picturesque than I'd expected. Whatever Bavarian charm the village might once have had was lost now in an ugly melange of newer buildings. The only thing missing was a McDonald's.

I stopped at a phone booth and checked the dirctory to see if Heidi Schultz was listed. She was. I scribbled her address on my palm and flagged down a taxi.

Ten minutes later I was knocking on her gingerbread front door.

The woman who answered was too young to be Heidi. Probably around 50. She was pretty in a motherly sort of way, and she spoke English fairly well. I introduced myself as John Stout, a Canadian entrepreneur, who wished to speak with Frau Schultz about "an extremely lucrative business venture."

"I'm sorry, she is not home," the woman said. "I am but the

housekeeper. Every day, this time, she goes up to the Nest. If you would please come back in perhaps two hours—"

"The Nest?"

She pointed to the nearest mountaintop—far from the tallest of the peaks, but one with quite a view—to an observatory built into the summit. "The Eagle's Nest," she said. "It is all that remains." She indicated a newer house, a large home, across the way. "That is where the Berghof stood. Now The Nest is all that is left. She goes up there at this time each day." She shrugged glumly. "It is her way."

"I see," I said. "There's an elevator...?"

She nodded toward a small building at the mountain's base. "The entrance is there. It is the only way up. There are no stairs."

"Well, I wouldn't want to disturb her reverie. Perhaps I will come back later."

"I will tell her you came. That you will return."

"By all means. Thank you."

As soon as she closed the door, I set out for the elevator.

The attendant there was earnest but not exactly security-minded. I told him that Frau Schultz was expecting me, and he sent me right up—but not before informing me in badly broken English that in the summer months the Nest was open as a public teahouse and that it was closed now, but Heidi had special access. He was probably the unfortunate, not-too-bright grandson of some Hitler loyalist, tucked away in this mundane yet patriotic job as a favor to his grandfather.

Heidi was startled when the elevator doors slid open and I stepped into the room. But she quickly regained her composure. "Who are you?" she said in easy English.

She was alone, sitting in one of several armchairs grouped around a small table by the window. Behind her stretched the now tiresome alpine panorama. She was small and plump but not fat.

I wondered what it was that had given me away as English-speaking.

"What do you want?" she asked.

Her face was deeply lined, her lips thin and bitter. Her hair was silver, with a residue of blonde, pulled tightly into a bun. She wore slacks and a ski jacket. It was chilly up there, even though it was summer.

"I'm sorry to disturb you, Frau Schultz," I said softly, reverentially, as if we were in a holy space. "My name is John Stout. I'm a businessman. From Toronto."

"I don't believe you," she said. "You look like a reporter."

"Frau Schultz, I can assure you that I am most certainly *not* a reporter. I am a businessman, and quite a successful one at that." I chuckled.

"Are you a Jew?"

"Methodist. Born and raised." The truth.

"You are not a Jew? One who has come to take revenge?"

"Nothing could be further from my mind." I looked around, again with an air of reverence. "So," I said, edging into the room, "this is where the great man came to take his afternoon tea. To relax with those he cared for. To unwind."

Tentatively, she said, "Yes. It was here. This was the place of the blue hour."

"Ah, yes. The blue hour. And you, Frau Schultz, were one of the lucky ones invited to join him." I sighed. "What I would have given to have been here as well."

"It was an honor to be in his presence. Always. To sit at his feet, to hear his wisdom. His jokes and wit." An off-kilter smile twisted her face. "He was a charmer who so loved the ladies. And I was but a young girl at the time. Still, I knew I was living in a moment of history. That whatever happened, I would treasure the memories for the rest of my life. And so it has been."

I had her. "Who can blame you? I wouldn't say this in public, for obvious reasons. The time is not right, not yet. Though it will be. But I can say to you what I've always believed in my heart. Adolf Hitler was the greatest of all the great men."

"It is true. To know him, to have been here, has made my life worth living. And to know him was to love him, as a popular song once said."

"I know the song well," I said. "The Ponytails, wasn't it?"

"The Teddy Bears. The Ponytails did 'Born Too Late.'"

"Yes, you're right."

"I'm sorry to nitpick," she said. "But the girl groups are a passion for me. Even if so many were concocted by the Jew Phil Spector. But the Jews do have talent. They can be a creative people. Even Hitler acknowledged that."

I'd always felt that Hitler's anti-Semitism had a strong personal component of envy and resentment over his rejection at the art school in Vienna, which he'd blamed on the Jews.

"Of course," Heidi said, "it's no accident that Spector himself once described his fabled Wall of Sound as 'Wagnerian.' Perhaps this is why I have always been so fond of it. Who can forget his masterwork, the Negress Tina Turner singing 'River Deep, Mountain High'?"

"I must say," I said, "I'm surprised to find a woman of your generation so knowledgeable on this subject."

"Well..." she looked sad, "I had a niece whose dream it was to be the German Lesley Gore."

"'It's My Party.'"

"I'm afraid the party ended quite abruptly for my Gisella. She was murdered by John Lennon."

"She was...?"

"Murdered. By John Lennon. Quite literally. She was clean and wholesome until the Beatles and John Lennon. She idolized John Lennon. And when he took LSD, she also took it. To be like him."

"So she knew him?"

"Of course not. She thought she did. She thought a lot of things. She thought she could fly. But instead she jumped from a mountaintop and fell to her death. Not far from here. By then she was a *hippie.*" She spat out the last word. "So when the boy shot Lennon, I felt that was justice."

"I understand," I said. *I understand that you are one twisted Nazi bitch.* "I understand perfectly."

"So what is it that I can do for you, Mr. Stout."

"Yes. Well, I'll cut to the chase. I've come a long way to see you, Frau Schultz, because I believe you may have information that I, as a businessman, might find quite profitable."

"Information?"

"The location of a cache of pills. Diet pills. Used by Eva Braun."

"Who told you this?"

"I spoke with Trevor Leland. Not long before he died."

"He is dead?" She was startled. "I did not know."

"That's understandable. He only died two days ago."

"He was murdered?"

"No, no. It appears to have been a heart attack."

"I see. Yes, I know he had a problem with his heart." She hesitated. "I cannot say this news brings me great sadness. I did not care for him. He was an evil man."

"I wasn't exactly fond of him myself. That book he wrote, in which he said that Hitler was a homosexual—"

"Rubbish!" she said. "Hitler loved women! And women loved him."

I sensed that *Frau Schultz* loved him.

"About the pills..."

"Eva took many pills," she said. "To sleep she took barbiturates, because of the constant bomb blasts. Sometimes I brought them to her. In the day she would take another kind of pill, phenobarbital, due to the stress. And she took pills from Dr. Morell, for what purpose I don't know. These might be the pills of which you speak."

"Yes," I said. "They very well might."

"Hitler himself took many pills from Dr. Morell, as well as cocaine for his sinus problem."

"Yes, I'd heard that." I felt myself getting impatient. "So, about the pills. Do you know where I could find them?"

"I can tell you where a supply of Eva's pills *might* be. But I can't tell you for sure that any pills are there or, if there are, that they are the pills you seek."

"Of course," I said.

"But I *can* tell you that if the pills you seek *are* there, then the information you seek is very valuable."

Capitalism: alive and well in Berchtesgaden. I smiled. "I can, of course, pay you for the information," I said. "Perhaps

$25,000 Canadian now, after you tell me where the pills might be, and then another $25,000 if I'm actually able to locate them."

"That is a generous offer, Mr. Stout. But the price is 2 million U.S. dollars. Firm. I couldn't part with Eva's legacy for any less. Not from Trevor. Not from you."

"Two million dollars?"

"Firm."

I suddenly grew tired of Frau Schultz.

I stepped forward and grabbed her by the neck. "Listen, bitch. Playtime's over. Where are the pills?"

What came out of her mouth next shocked me. "Why don't you lick my ass, Jew."

I realized I was dealing with one sick Nazi cooze.

I dragged her to the picture window, which I'd already scoped out. It had a latch, which I flipped. The entire window opened inward—the only way to have washed its outside face. As I pulled it back, its hinges squeaked and an icy alpine wind swept the room.

She was actually quite small, despite her plumpness, and old. It wasn't hard to push her to the window ledge. Below was a straight drop of 100 feet or so, then jagged rocks and another drop.

"Tell me where the pills are and convince me you're not lying," I said. "Or out you go, you rancid piece of Nazi shit."

"Go ahead, kill me," she said. "I will die someday soon anyway."

I sighed. And twisted her brittle arm behind her back. "OK, bitch. Play games if you want. Let's see how you like excruciating pain."

She shrieked as I twisted her arm toward the breaking point.

"Talk and I'll stop. Don't talk and this is just the beginning."

"I will talk!"

I quit twisting her arm, but I kept a tight grip on her. And kept her by the open window, a nudge away from death. "Spill it."

"The pills are in the bunker."

"What bunker?"

"*The* bunker. The Führerbunker! In Berlin."

"Bullshit," I said. "There is no Führerbunker. The Russians blew it up after the war, so people like you wouldn't make it a shrine."

"No," she said. "Only the entrance. It was sealed off, you see. But the bunker still exists."

I had heard something about this. I hadn't paid much attention to the story at the time. But I did recall that after reunification it had been discovered that the Führerbunker hadn't been as thoroughly destroyed as was once believed.

Given that, I said to Heidi, "Fine. Where exactly in the bunker are the pills?"

"In the sofa. The...the...love seat! The love seat."

"The love seat in the Führerbunker. How incongruous."

"Eva hid pills there. Sometimes she would hide extra pills in the love seat. For when Dr. Morell wasn't around."

"And where exactly in the bunker is this love seat?"

"In Hitler's private room. It was on this love seat that he and Eva took their lives. He with a pistol, she with a cyanide pellet."

"So what are you telling me? That the love seat's been sitting there for over 50 years? That Eva spilled some pills into the cracks between the cushions?"

"I did not say the pills would be there. Only that they *might* be there. I only learned of the restoration a short time ago. I have not been there."

"The restoration?"

"Yes. The bunker has been restored."

"By whom?"

Nothing.

I twisted her arm again. Hard.

"Baldur Schenk!" she cried.

"The furniture guy?"

She nodded.

Schenk owned a hugely successful home furnishings chain, essentially a German version of IKEA. He was a handsome and popular European media figure, with a stunning wife, a bent for "new" German nationalism, and unspecified political ambitions. His father, Otto Schenk, had been a controversial architect during the Nazi period. As a member of Albert Speer's design team, Otto had initially garnered Hitler's favor, until something—the stories varied—went terribly awry, and Otto spent the duration of the war years in prison. Before that, though, he'd named his son after his close friend, Hitler Youth leader Baldur Von Schirach. And there were persistent rumors that the younger Schenk, despite his father's ill treatment by Hitler, was a closet Nazi. All of which is a way of saying that Heidi's story made more sense than I wished.

"So you're telling me that Baldur Schenk restored the Führerbunker? How?"

"He has a store. How do you say it? *Eine grossen—*"

"A megastore?"

"Yes, that's it. He has a megastore on the Wilhelmstrasse. Quite close to the site of the bunker."

"And there's a way to reach the bunker from the store?"

"Yes. But I have not seen it."

"Let me be clear on this," I said. "The furniture, including the love seat, was down there in the bunker all these years? Until Baldur—"

"No, no. It was all removed in 1945. It was stored by the Russians, and later by the East Germans, I don't know where. But Baldur has put everything back just as it was. Down to the smallest detail. In Hitler's private room: the love seat, the carpets, the portrait of Frederick the Great on the wall..."

I didn't actually want to believe any of this. Because if I did, I'd feel compelled to pursue it—less for Diane's sake than my own. But my gut was telling me there might be something going on here. It seemed far-fetched—the whole idea. On the other hand, Heidi knew too much to be making it all up on the spot.

"May I infer from all of this," I said, "that you're on speaking terms with Baldur?"

"Oh, yes. I can tell you—" She censored herself.

"That's OK. I can finish the sentence. He loves Hitler as much as you do."

She flashed a snaky smile. "If you think I'm going to call him and get you an invitation to the bunker—"

"That's *exactly*," and here I gave another hard twist to her arm, "what you're going to do."

"Why?" she cried. "So you can kill me once I've made the call?"

"I won't do that."

"You're right. You won't. But only because I won't let you," she said, and wrenched herself free.

I knew what she intended to do, and I didn't try to stop her.

"This is quite right," she said. "I love this place. I love this place beyond any on earth." And then she jumped through the open window.

Like mother, like daughter.

I stepped to the window and looked down at her body, splayed on the rocks far below. "River deep, *liebchen.* Mountain high."

I left quickly, knowing her body would soon be discovered.

I nodded to the attendant and smiled as I exited the elevator.

He smiled in return. "Did you have a nice visit?"

"Yes," I said. "Very nice."

Two hours later I was on a Lufthansa flight from Munich to Berlin, traveling this time on a fake U.S. passport as Robert Barber, a history professor from Santa Barbara.

The next afternoon I was sitting in a pale brown calfskin chair in Baldur Schenk's large office. He was sitting in a similar, higher-backed chair at a massive glass desk that held nothing more than a legal pad, a pen, and a multiline telephone. Behind him were plate-glass windows overlooking the vast showroom—the *extremely* vast showroom—of his Wilhelmstrasse megastore, where yuppie Berliners wandered through a complicated maze of room displays.

Appearance-wise, Schenk was a knockoff of the British

actor Terence Stamp—fine features, tan skin, silver hair—a dashing former pretty boy who had aged extremely well. His dark blue suit was as immaculate as his birch-paneled office.

"So, the Führerbunker, Professor Barber," he said to me from across the room. "You have come here from..."

"Santa Barbara," I said. "In California."

"Yes, Santa Barbara. You have come here all the way from Santa Barbara to ask me about the Führerbunker."

This was how I'd gotten in. I'd simply asked the guard at the downstairs desk to call Schenk's office and let them know I was there with some research questions about "the current state of the Führerbunker." I'd been pretty sure this would do the trick, and I hadn't been disappointed.

"Yes, Herr Schenk," I said. "Let me come straight to the point. Because I can see, of course, that you're a very busy man."

"This is true."

I should mention that I was subtly dorking out. Irritating him somewhat seemed like the best strategy, so he'd go along with my wish just to get rid of me. So in my mind I was channeling Jerry Lewis. Not too much, though. Not over-the-top. But enough to make him view me as harmless and tedious.

"Very well, Herr Schenk, I am writing a book on the last days of Adolf Hitler." I held up my hand. "Oh, I know what you're thinking. This has been done. And done and done and done. But most of these books, perhaps *all* of them, are trash. Pseudohistory, Herr Schenk. Books for the masses. As opposed to the *scholarly* work I am undertaking."

He was keeping his cool. But I could tell I was setting his teeth on edge. "I see. What I don't understand, though,

Professor Barber, is why you think I can be of help with this matter."

I leaned forward in my chair, but it still felt as if he was 50 feet away. "It is my understanding that the bunker was located no more than a quarter kilometer from where we are sitting. A quarter kilometer and of course *down.* In fact," I gestured to the showroom floor below, "directly below what is now your children's furniture department."

"You are quite correct, Professor Barber. May I inquire as to how you've come across this information?"

"I'm afraid I'm not at liberty to reveal my source. But I can tell you it is someone who would have access to such information."

"And what else has this source told you?"

"Let's just say I have reason to believe that Adolf Hitler and Eva Braun did *not* commit suicide in the bunker. That the suicides were faked, and that Hitler and Eva escaped into the sewers through a secret exit in Hitler's private sitting room or bedroom. And that they lived the remainder of their years in Paraguay, then Argentina, and finally Chile."

Schenk allowed himself a cocky chuckle. "Preposterous."

"That was my first reaction as well. However—"

"Hitler died in the bunker." Here, his anger flashed. As I'd hoped. "He had many chances to escape, but he stayed. He was not a coward. He would not slither like a rat through a sewer into hiding." He saw what he was doing and collected himself. Calm again, he said, "There is no such tunnel, I assure you."

"Yes, well, I was hoping you could *show* me."

"I will show you," he said. "But only after you tell me the identity of your source."

"Well, you've probably guessed anyway. Heidi Schultz."

He laughed to himself, as if at a private joke. "Ah, yes. Heidi." Abruptly he stood. "Come, I have a meeting in a short while. Let me show you what you want to see, so you may put these lies to rest."

He led me from his office, around a couple of corners and down different corridors, until we came to an elevator with an optic sensor. Waiting there were two men. A large, chunky blond who reminded me of Gert Fröbe, the actor who played Goldfinger in the Bond film. He struck me as an obvious bodyguard. His companion, though, wasn't so obvious: a skinny, suited fellow with sharp, rodent features—reminiscent of Goebbels. Schenk peered into the dark glass of the sensor, and the elevator doors immediately and silently opened.

On the way down, a lengthy descent, the big guy was introduced as Klaus. Ratface remained nameless. Schenk surprised me by volunteering information in an oddly offhand tone. "You know, when this place was first rediscovered, it was quite a mess. For decades there was nothing above it but an empty field. Then, after reunification, hooligans uncovered the main entrance to the bunker. For a while it was open to anyone and everyone. So it was defiled. Used as a cheap shrine. It was a desecration that had to stop. This is why I built my store here and bought up all the nearby land."

"I'm so glad," I said. "It's an important piece of history. There's no getting around that. Whatever people think of Hitler, and I personally feel he was a very complex man, it's extremely important that future generations be able to see a site such as this intact."

"Precisely my feelings, Professor Barber."

"I must confess, Herr Schenk, I feel a little shiver up my spine. I can't tell you how much—"

"It's not a problem."

When the elevator stopped, the doors opened into a concrete stairwell. Schenk switched on the lights—ceiling bulbs set in cages. A bright, oppressive glow. He led the way down the stairway to the lowest level. Klaus and Ratface made me nervous. I started to worry that this had all gone too smoothly.

"The official dining room is one floor above," Schenk said as we stepped into a long, narrow room on the bottom floor. "But Hitler often used this room for more intimate gatherings."

Indeed, a long wooden table took up the entire center of the room, with mismatched chairs—which surprised me—around it. Barren but clean, the room had a fresh-scrubbed appearance, which didn't take away the strong odor of mildew. Probably nothing could, at this point. The bare concrete walls, rough with wood-frame imprints, glistened with moisture.

"This is where Hitler dined with his closest staff members," Schenk said. "And it was here, the day before he died, that he married Eva Braun. As you can see, this room is not yet finished. It once had wood panels and Italian paintings. But the wood became wet and rotted over time. Elsewhere, however, the restoration is complete."

He opened a door. "Now I will show you what you wish to see." We stepped through a small foyer, and another door, and there it was. Hitler's sitting room, much smaller than I'd expected. But there it stood, fully restored. The room's pine paneling had been replaced, and a Persian carpet covered most of the concrete floor. A small writing table held a framed photo of Hitler's homely mother. On the wall hung Hitler's cherished (and cheesy) portrait of Frederick the Great. And there was the settee.

I spotted two other doors, both metal, and both ajar, revealing glimpses of two bedrooms: Hitler's and Eva's, I assumed.

But my attention was focused on the settee, with its fresh, rose-patterned upholstery. Much too fresh, and devoid of bloodstains. As fresh as the furniture upstairs in Baldur Schenk's showroom.

I commented with an air of awe. "So this is where he is supposed to have died."

"This is where he *did* die."

"It appears you've had this reupholstered." I pointed to the love seat.

"Unfortunately, this piece is not original. That was lost many years ago. This is a replica. Quite accurate, though, down to the smallest detail."

"Impressive," I said.

"*This,* however," Schenk said, "is the genuine article." He held a Walther semiautomatic pistol in his hand. And he was aiming it at me.

I took a feeble stab at innocence. "You mean, that's the actual gun he used to—"

"Yes." He stepped in closer. "And it's also the one that's going to put a hole in *your* head unless you tell me who you *really* are. Now," he said, "start talking. Who sent you? Who are you working for?"

"I don't know what you mean. I've told you, I wanted to see if there's a tunnel."

Schenk threw open the door to Hitler's bedroom, lovingly restored, complete with a swastika-emblazoned bedspread. "See," he said. "No door. Now, who are you? Who sent you to kill me?"

"Excuse me?"

"For whom did you kill Frau Schultz?" With that, he back-handed me, which shocked me more than it hurt. "She was seen yesterday with a supposed Canadian matching your description."

I was as scared as I'd ever been. "I...I..."

To Klaus and Ratface, he said, "Take him into the dining room. I will not defile this spot."

Klaus reached into his jacket pocket and produced a pair of ordinary household pliers. He and his boss spoke briefly in German. I know enough German that I got the gist. Klaus was going to work on my testicles.

Hoden is German for "testicles."

I instinctively reacted, lunging at Schenk and wrenching the pistol out of his hand. I jammed it under his chin, spun, and used him for a shield.

I'd guessed correctly that Ratface was armed. He was reaching for his gun when I said, "Don't touch it or I'll blow his fucking head off!"

Schenk chimed in as well. "Dieter, *nein.*" And in English for my benefit, "Do what he says."

Trying not to spaz on adrenaline, I said, "All right. You two, into the bedroom," nodding toward Hitler's room.

Klaus and Dieter stayed frozen until Schenk told them

again, this time in German, to do as I said.

"Dieter," I said. "Take your gun out, very carefully, and put it on the table."

He removed a nine-millimeter pistol from a shoulder holster and placed it on the end table, next to the settee.

"Now, into the bedroom."

Both men backed into Hitler's sleeping quarters. I moved Schenk to the door, which I closed. I turned the key in the lock, all the while keeping the Walther pressed to Schenk's chin.

"All right," I said. "Now let's talk."

"What for? What can I tell you that you don't already know?"

"I want to know what happened to the original of that." I indicated the settee.

"What? You must be kidding."

"Hardly," I said. "You said the original furniture was lost. What happened to it?"

"What are you? Some kind of sociopathic art dealer?"

I jammed the gun deeper into his chin. "What happened to the love seat?"

"If I knew, it would be here," he said. "I tried to find it when I first began this restoration. Do you see that lamp?" He meant a brass pole lamp with a green cloth shade. "That is the original. We traced it to St. Petersburg. There is a rumor that Stalin kept the settee himself. As a souvenir. If it was so, then the settee disappeared with Stalin's death."

"But in theory, it could still exist," I said. "In someone's private collection. Or stuck away in storage in some Russian barn somewhere."

"Anything is possible," he said.

Indeed. And that included the accidental discharge of a 50-

plus-year-old Walther pistol. Which is what happened next, to my shock and Schenk's. To Klaus's and Dieter's too.

The bullet, which for all I know had been resting in the chamber since 1945, tore through Schenk's chin and lodged, it's safe to guess, in his brain. There was no exit wound, thank God, or I'd have been covered in blood and bone fragments and brain tissue.

Still, there was quite a lot of blood from his chin, and it spilled onto the fresh new settee where I lowered him. He gurgled and jerked and expired within seconds. In the same room, in much the same way as his idol more than 50 years earlier.

When my ears stopped ringing, I heard Klaus and Dieter attacking the iron door and yelling in German.

"It was an accident," I yelled. "I swear."

And then I wiped my prints off the gun and got the fuck out.

I left Berlin as quickly as possible, hoping to escape before Klaus and Dieter got out of Hitler's bedroom. I lucked out, catching an Air France flight to Moscow, where I checked into the Hilton and slept for 11 hours straight.

In the morning, over a room service breakfast, I placed a call to a friend who teaches European history at a prestigious American university and is an expert on Stalin. It took me less than five minutes to find out what I needed to know.

I asked, "When Stalin died in '53, do you know who got his furniture?"

"Which furniture?" he drawled. Although he speaks fluent Russian and several other languages, he has a deep Southern accent. "From which home? He had several."

I narrowed my search. "All right, let me ask you this. Have you ever heard anything about Stalin having had in his possession the sofa on which Hitler killed himself? You know, the settee from the Führerbunker?"

"Oh, sure. Yeah, he had that. Kept it in his *dacha,* the one south of Moscow. Liked to show it off."

"I see," I said. "Do you know what happened to that sofa when he died?"

"Sure. His niece got it. She hated the damn thing. Gave her the willies. Put it in storage with some other stuff. As far as I know, it's still there."

"She's still alive, then?"

"Oh, sure. She's not much older than we are. Geta Gogol. That's her married name. Her husband's a descendant of the writer. She's been a real gold mine."

"I can imagine."

"So why are you looking for this, anyway? Don't tell me you want to run a DNA test on the bloodstains to make sure they're really his."

I laughed. "No, nothing so upstanding. A collector wants it, and he's willing to pay a substantial finder's fee. If it's in good condition."

"Well, you'd have to ask Geta about that."

"I'd like to. Any idea where she is?"

"Not far from you, actually. And I've got a feeling she'll deal if she's got it. She hasn't exactly flourished since the Soviet breakup, if you catch my drift. I'd give you her phone number, but the last time I tried it, it'd been shut off. Probably couldn't pay her bill. But I've got the address here somewhere..."

Within an hour I was boarding a train for Kharkov, which turned out to be a small, rundown village about 80 kilometers southeast of Moscow. From the Kharkov station, I took a taxi to Geta Gogol's address, a seedy *dacha* on a bad road in thick woods. As I walked up the driveway, I saw her waiting for me on the porch.

She was in her mid 40s, heavyset, but pretty in a puffy-faced way. She wore a floral dress and a frilly apron, attire that seemed like a throwback to the 1950s. I started to introduce myself. "Hello, I'm—"

"Yes, I know who you are, Mr. James Baker. I get phone call from," and here she named my academic friend. "My phone cut off, but he find my new number. I would call you in Moscow, to save you this trouble, but is too expensive. You understand?"

"I'm not sure."

She nodded. "You have come a long way. Please, I make you tea."

I followed her inside, into a dark living room filled with crappy furniture. She appeared to live alone. She confirmed this as I followed her into the kitchen, where she put water on to boil.

"My husband die last year," she said. "From the chemicals. You understand?"

"Yes, I think so." I presumed she meant cancer caused by exposure to either radiation or chemicals. "I'm sorry."

"It is not easy," she said. "If I had this thing you want, the

Hitler couch, I would sell it gladly. It always gave me...what's the word?"

"The creeps?"

"Creeps. Yes, I think that is the word. It sounds right." She smiled faintly.

"What happened to the couch, Mrs. Gogol?"

She looked out the window, indicating a dilapidated guest house. "You see? We use that for storage. For many years, the couch is there. Then six, seven years ago, a bad rain comes. The roof is leaking. We don't know, since only for storage. The rain stops, and we find much damage. The couch no good. So we throw it out."

"I see," I said, disappointed.

"Too wet. No good."

"I understand."

On the stove the teapot whistled. She poured the boiling water into a ceramic pot over loose tea leaves and left it to steep. I sat at the kitchen table, deflated. After all this, after feeling so close. And now nothing.

Then she stepped into the dining room, where I heard her open a cabinet. "This person who want the couch," she said. "Do you think he would pay for these?"

She came back to the kitchen and placed an aged Cuban cigar box on the table. Its faded, illustrated label read, "Eldorado." "I clean the couch once many years ago and find these things under the pillows."

I flipped open the box: several vintage bobby pins, some coins from the 1930s and '40s, a tarnished brass lipstick tube. I opened the tube. Cherry red, dried and cracked, but intact. Next there was a yellowed scrap of paper with some names scrawled on it in a shaky hand: Bormann, T. Junge, J. und M. Goebbels... *A guest list for the wedding?* And finally there was a dark brown glass pill bottle. The label was faded almost to the point of illegibility. But I could still make out the name—Eva Braun—and date—February 23, 1945.

I shook the bottle.

There were pills inside.

I unscrewed the cap and poured the pills into my hand. They were small, round, pale green, and hard as pebbles.

"The bitch like red," Geta said, pointing to the lipstick.

"Yes," I said. "Bitches often do like red." Nancy Reagan came to mind.

"You think someone pay for these things?" Geta asked.

"Yes, I think so." I stayed cool. "This is almost surely Eva Braun's lipstick." I picked up the paper. "And I would guess that this is Hitler's handwriting. Just from the scrawl. He had palsy at that point, I think."

"I will sell these to you for 600,000 rubles." Approximately $10,000.

I was already digging into my satchel. "I'll give you $1,500 U.S. for the things. And another $500 if you'll promise to not tell anyone I was here."

She took the money and shrugged. "I have no reason to. Is not like the old days. The police did not follow?"

"No. I watched."

"No one follow?"

"No one."

"Is not like the old days."

Ⓐ

I climbed out of the taxi in front of the Hilton, as if I were Cary Grant in a Russian remake of *North by Northwest—North by Northeast*?—when a thug in a trench coat approached me from behind and stuck a gun, concealed in his jacket, in the small of my back. "Get into the black car," he said.

An ugly, boxy, Soviet-era sedan.

The Hilton doorman was preoccupied with some arriving guests, oblivious to my situation.

I had no options. I climbed into the passenger seat of the piece of shit car, only to see *another* piece of shit: Vlad. The thug with the gun joined Vlad in the backseat, and the driver hit the gas.

Vlad leaned toward me and said, inches from my face, "Hello, fuck."

His breath stank of vodka.

"Vlad!" I said. "Small world, isn't it?"

"Fuck you, you fuck. I had to leave the States because it got so hot. They call me back here, and I think I will never get you. And then you come to me! Ha!" He seemed genuinely amused.

"Yes," I said feyly. "So tell me, how *did* you find me?"

"I sit in the fucking bar at the fucking Hilton with a friend, and into the fucking hotel you walk. I fucking watched you check fucking in. You stupid fucking asshole."

"Well, what do you know? That *is* one for the books."

"I check with the desk, see you have a fake fucking name. But I know your fucking face when I see it, fuckface."

"Yes, right. You know, Vlad, fuck is a fine word, heaven knows. But I'm afraid it starts to lose a bit of its punch when—"

"Shut up, fuck. I don't want to hear your fucking bullshit. So just fucking shut the fuck up. We're almost there."

There turned out to be an abandoned meat market.

We parked in front on a scuzzy street, and the thug with the gun steered me inside, Vlad and the driver close behind.

"Into the back," Vlad ordered.

We stepped past the empty meat cases into the butcher's room, where the floor was still bloodstained. The room itself gave off the rank odor of, well, dead meat. Which is what I figured I was, even if I coughed up the O.J. tape. I knew how much Vlad hated me at that point. Enough to take his time with me.

The thug with the gun pulled me toward a table housing a huge buzz saw, designed to cut through meat and bone like a hot knife in warm butter. He flipped the switch, and the blade began to spin. Smoothly, with a high-pitched whine. Dying with dignity was going to be very difficult.

"I ask you just once," Vlad said, "and then I cut off your fucking fingers and your fucking toes. Fucking one at a time. Then I cut off your dick and stuff it down your fucking throat so you fucking suffocate. Then I cut off your head with your dick stuffed into it, and fucking mail it to..." Apparently, he couldn't think of anyone to mail it to. "Fuck it. I will feed it to rats. I will feed your fucking head and cock to rats." He paused. "I ask you one time. Where is the fucking tape?"

"OK," I said. "I'll tell you. But the tape is less than worthless. I wasn't kidding when I told you it's a fake."

"I know that, you stupid fuck. But it's a perfect fake. That's what your asshole friend told me. Before I do my number."

"It's flawed," I said. I knew I was running out of time. "The tape is worthless, but if you look in my satchel, you'll find a cigar box containing some very interesting items."

The driver picked up my satchel and dumped its contents onto a bloodstained tabletop. Vlad sorted through the items and found the cigar box. I hoped he wouldn't find the cash tucked in the bag's false bottom.

Meanwhile, the saw continued to whine.

It was now or never. Vlad and the driver were focused on the contents of my luggage. The thug with the gun was the only one watching me, and he was distracted by the actions of his comrades. I spun on him and shoved his arm into the blade, slicing it off smoothly just below the elbow.

He howled, his blood flying everywhere. *Spurting.* Like in a horror film.

I grabbed his gun—a small machine pistol—from the hand of his severed arm.

Then all hell broke loose. As I'd more or less expected, Vlad and the driver were also armed. As they reached for their shoulder-holstered weapons, I sprayed them, catching Vlad in the center of the forehead with a round that made a hole the size of a dime.

Then it was over, except for the howling amputee on the floor, who'd somehow escaped the hail of gunfire. Vlad and the driver had fallen in twisted heaps. I was stunned and reeling.

I collected myself. I also collected my things, which I stuffed back into my satchel.

All the while, the thug on the floor was screaming his head off.

By the time I got back to L.A., I was beat. I went directly to the Vault, collapsed into bed, and slept for 15 hours.

Then I called Diane Rainey. "I've got what you want."

She sucked in her breath. "Say no more. Come right over."

Diane was plopped in the same spot on the couch she'd been in on my last visit. I wondered if she'd even gotten up while I was gone. She took the brown glass pill bottle from my outstretched hand and read the label in awe. "My God," she said. "You did it. You found it. My husband thinks you're an asshole, but I told him—" She stopped herself.

"That's OK. I think he's an asshole too."

I waited for her reaction, but she was scrutinizing the pills. She'd emptied them from the bottle into her palm.

"Don't take them all at once," I said.

"Ha, ha," she said. "Is this all there is?" She counted the pills. "Seven?"

"There were 14. I kept half."

"You *kept* some of the pills? I don't remember discussing that."

"I don't think we did discuss it in so many words. But I'm going to do the same thing you are. I'm going to have them analyzed so I'll know what they are. And don't forget, peaches, you still owe me $250,000, which I would like right now by the way. And the formula is mine exclusively. That's the deal."

"Well..." She examined the pills closely. "I've been thinking about that."

"Yeah? Why am I not surprised?"

"Don't jump to conclusions. I'm still prepared to pay you. As soon as I'm sure these are legitimate. That they're not little German mints or something."

"I don't think they're mints, Diane. Now, tell me what's on your mind."

I watched her struggle for the right words.

"Just that, if these pills are what we hope, it might make sense for everyone, including you, Jim, if we...if we went into business together."

"Not a snowball's chance in hell, Diane."

"James, hear me out. I think you'll see this is the obvious thing to do. Biff and I have the money and the connections to launch a product like this in *just* the right way. We might want to sell it on TV, for example. I'd never do infomercials myself, of course. I'm too big a star."

I refrained from commenting.

She continued on, oblivious. "I do, however, know people who have no qualms about that sort of thing. Like Cher. Like Suzanne Somers. I just don't think you have the resources to do something like that. And you'd still be making millions. What more do you want?"

She was radically changing the terms of our deal. But she did have a point. "Get your pills analyzed," I said. "And I'll do the same with mine. And if they're something that might actually work, we'll talk."

"That's fine," she said. "I already have a lab that's prepared to do the testing."

"I want my 250 grand either way."

"That's understandable. I only asked for the pills. I couldn't expect you to know if they're any good." She poured the pills back into the bottle. "As soon as I'm sure these are real, that they're 50 years old and some sort of plausible weight-loss formulation, you'll be paid."

Plausible? Hmm. "How soon will that be?"

"I'll call you."

It wasn't what I wanted to hear, but it *was* what I'd expected—including her revision of the deal. Which didn't bother me all that much, since I couldn't really see myself stuck behind the CEO's desk of Miracle Quick Lose Fat Corp.

I drove straight to a lab in the Valley, a place where I knew the owner, who'd done some work for me before—both drug and HIV testing. I'll call him Dwayne. I knew I could trust him.

I'd put the seven pills into an unmarked plastic pill bottle, but I told Dwayne, "These are about 50 years old."

"I can see that." He'd poured the pills into a tray under a bright lab light.

"You think you can tell me what's in them?"

He picked up one of the pills with tweezers and looked at it closely. "Oh yeah. This kind of coating is hard as a clamshell.

If you'd found these in a pharaoh's tomb, the contents would be just as intact as the day they were made. I *will* have to open these very carefully. Once you let the air in... Where the hell did these come from?"

"Can't really tell you, Dwayne. How long will it take?"

"Depends on how complex the formula is. If we're looking at a single drug, I may be able to tell you right away. But if we've got a combo, it could take a few days. Or longer."

"Well, the sooner you can find out..."

"I'll keep you posted."

I said, "I appreciate it, Dwayne." But he didn't hear me, already preoccupied with the pills and their contents.

A few minutes after I got back to the Vault, my cell phone rang. "Yeah?"

"Is this Jim?" Male voice, probably in his 20s. He sounded frightened.

"Who wants to know?"

"Look, my name is...my name is Steve. You don't know me, but I was a friend of Ken's. That's how I have your number. I'm a video director. Music videos. Anyway, here's the thing. I've got a copy of the tape. The, uh, *juicy* tape you gave to Ken. He wanted me to have it in case something happened to him. And as we know, something did."

"Go on," I said.

"OK. Well, I know Ken thought the tape was real. But I know for a fact it isn't."

"What makes you think that?"

"Well, it's very convincing. But it's wrong. The, uh, throat slash is wrong. That's not how it happened. They messed up on that."

"They?"

"That's why I'm calling you. I know who made the tape."

"I see," I said. "Who?"

"I can't tell you over the phone. I mean, I'm not comfortable with that. I've probably said too much already."

"Are you saying you'd like to meet in person?"

"I think that would be better. I'd feel safer."

The fear in his voice rang true. But given the assortment of people trying to kill me, I said, "I think *I* would feel safer doing this over the phone."

"I can't do that. Look, I understand why you're paranoid. I'm just a voice on the phone. But this is for real. This isn't a setup. I'm very frightened right now because of what I know. And what they did to Ken..."

My instinct told me he was almost certainly for real. I knew I had to take a chance. "I'll meet you in a public place. How's that?"

"Fine. Of course, that's fine. The sooner the better."

We agreed to meet on the busy Third Street Promenade in Santa Monica, in front of the Midnight Special bookstore.

Steve was waiting when I got there. Late 20s, short brown hair, goatee. Baggy, faded jeans, Jesus Lizard T-shirt.

Scared green eyes. He had a camcorder with him.

"I'm Jim," I said.

"I know. I recognize you from your book photos."

The promenade, as usual, was crowded with a mix of students, nuevo-hipsters, yuppies, and sun-charred homeless people. Steve lifted his camera so I could look at the playback on the viewfinder screen. "Just to show I'm for real."

On the screen I watched O.J. stab Ron. It was the tape all right.

"OK," I said.

He shut it off. "Can we walk?"

"Sure." It was a nice day.

We headed north toward Wilshire Boulevard. His eyes were darting everywhere. I knew I had to calm him down. "So," I said, "you make videos. Anything I would know?"

"If you've seen MTV, you've seen my work." He mentioned some groups he'd worked for, most of them well-known, and in fact I knew one of his videos well.

"That one's creepy," I said, which I meant as a compliment.

"I hear that a lot. I get confused with Anton Corbijin." A soft laugh. "Which isn't a bad thing."

"So, um, you mentioned that you know who made the tape?"

He waited until a pack of teens passed. "A religious group. In Tennessee. A cult, really, called Genesis. Rabid fundamentalist Christians. They have a lab near Nashville. It's part of a compound. They tape a bunch of shows there that play on the Jesus Channel."

It's not really called the Jesus Channel. But I knew which one he meant.

"And how is it that you know this?"

"Because...I worked there. Briefly. Last month."

I thought about his creepy video, which was clogged with imagery most fundies would consider sacrilegious and obscene. "You worked there?"

"Making videos."

"Like the juicy one."

"Let me explain," he said. "About three months ago I had a crisis. I was strung out. On speed, to be specific. Crystal. It was bad. I was starting to go psychotic, but I couldn't stop taking it. And then one night I was alone and I'd been up for several days, and I was watching TV, and I was vulnerable. And I clicked to the Jesus Channel, and you've got to understand that I was out of my mind. It was one of those shows where they get messages from God about people in pain and trouble. And this preacher, he said, 'I feel someone in California with a drug problem, a serious amphetamine addiction, who's in great pain, but very close to Jesus, very close to Christ's salvation, if he will only call.' And there was an 800 number. You can fill in the rest."

"I see."

"I mean, I was in great pain, and I needed something to help me get straight. And it did. And for a while I bought into it. I accepted Jesus into my heart and all that. And it really helped. My cravings went away. And when the Genesis people found out who I was, that I was a successful video maker, they flew me out to Tennessee. They said that even though I'd been using my talents for Satan, I could repent and use them for Jesus." He was still glancing around with every step. "After a while my mind cleared and I saw what they were really about. And I knew I had to get out of there."

"So you don't consider yourself a born-again now?"

"Fuck, no." For the first time I heard anger in his voice. "They're vile. They're pigs. That's why I'm telling you this. They need to be exposed and destroyed."

"You're sure they made the O.J. tape?"

"Absolutely. And there's more on the way."

"Meaning...?"

Here, he really looked around. "I was working on another tape. This is why I'm scared. This is why I'm stalling them. They still think I'm coming back. Because...I was working on another tape."

"Another tape?"

"Of Hillary Clinton having sex with Vince Foster. And then shooting him."

"Are you kidding?"

"I wish I were. It's shot through windows so it looks like a surveillance tape. That's the idea. To make it look like something shot by detectives or the FBI. A tape that was shot and suppressed or whatever. Except this copy will surface."

"Jesus."

"They're scared of her running for president. And that's not all they've got planned. And as you know, they're good. The Hillary tape, once it's done, *will* pass inspection."

"Jesus fucking Christ." I checked him out closely. "You're not setting me up, are you? This isn't all horseshit, is it? Tell me the truth: Are you working for either a German modular furniture retailer or the Russian Mafia?"

"What?"

I smiled. "Forget it."

"You know," he said, "I don't live that far from here. Just over by Montana." Now *he* smiled. "The street. Not the state."

For a moment I hesitated, knowing his invitation could be a trap. But then I imagined his body beneath his baggy clothes. He wasn't gym-pumped, but he'd be firm. With light hair on his subtly defined chest and in a line down his flat stomach. And he had a plain, masculine face, the kind I like.

He smiled again, self-consciously.

"Sure," I said. "That sounds nice."

Once I saw Steve's apartment in an old, Spanish-style building on Sixth Street, it was clear that he was who he said he was: a music video director, aspiring feature director, and serious film buff. Video equipment clogged the place—not unlike Ken's apartment—and vintage movie posters covered the walls: *Touch of Evil, Gun Crazy, The Big Heat.*

"I'm going to move one of these days," he said as he brought me some iced tea. "My accountant says I should buy a house and all that. But it's been hard to give up this place. You know, rent control."

We sat on the sofa, but we weren't there for long. We started making out, then took it into the bedroom, where we got naked under a huge poster for *Vertigo.* His body was just as I'd imagined.

Afterward, we lay in bed talking for a long time—first about private matters, our past breakups. Then more about Genesis, the place in Tennessee.

"You really think this Hillary tape will pass inspection?"

"Definitely," he said. "They're good. Or I should say *Ray* is good. He's the true genius. He got rich designing software. Programs like Premiere. Until he found Jesus. I guess he's kind of what they were hoping I'd become. If I'd stayed. If I were to go back, I'd be working closely with Ray again."

"You're not thinking about going back, are you?" The prospect alarmed me.

He smiled softly. "No way. Especially not if I can see you again."

PART TWO
THE MIKE YANAGITA INTERLUDE

Steve spent the next several days and nights with me in the Palisades. He didn't feel safe at his place, and I didn't feel safe *anywhere* except the Vault. It was during this time that we hatched a plan for me to infiltrate Genesis—a plan that required a crash course in computer graphics from Steve. We used Phil's computer, which was pretty high-end and had all the basic graphics software. We had everything we needed for me to learn the ropes right there in our snug safe house. And when we weren't at the keyboard, we had a lot of fun—of different kinds. The sex was extremely gratifying, and I was starting to like Steve in a lot of other ways too. I told him as much.

"You wouldn't like me on speed," he said.

That was the only good thing about the born-again debacle, he felt. It had kept him off speed long enough that he now felt, cautiously, that he'd broken the back of the addiction. He admitted that sometimes he still had random urges and even dreamed at night of using speed. It had only been a few months since he'd stopped, after all. "It's like smoking, I guess. You have a moment of craving, then it passes."

We were discussing this one afternoon over a light lunch on the terrace when my cell phone rang. It was Linkletter.

He said, "Are you sitting down?"

"Cut the shit, Frank."

"You know Patti Grant?"

The *Sea Crew* starlet. Billy Seavers' original target.

"Not personally. But I don't know Barbie either."

"Don't laugh," he said. "This is no joke. You know that Miss Grant has had some plastic surgery."

Patti Grant had the most famous fake rack on the planet.

"Almost all of the work was done by one doctor," he said. "A guy named Donald Herschman."

"Plastic surgeon to the stars," I said. "When I was thinking of a butt tuck a while back, I almost—"

"Listen, this is serious. Herschman did her face, her butt, he liposuctioned this and that. Tummy tuck, whatever."

"And...?"

"And her tits, obviously."

"I hear she can't stay in the sun too long or the silicone will melt."

"That's sort of the problem," he said. "It's not all silicone."

"Meaning...?"

"I'm coming to that. Apparently there were something like 19 separate surgeries. He spent a long time on her face. New chin, nose, eye work, cheek implants, what have you. A relationship developed."

"You mean they were fucking?"

"Well, *that* I'm not sure about. But he definitely became obsessed with her."

"So what's the problem with her tits?"

"Within each implant, there's also a charge of C-4 plastique and a tiny detonation device."

"Her tits are *bombs*?"

At this point, Steve, who'd been listening, said, "*What*?"

I shushed him, then said to Linkletter, "Tell me this has a punch line."

"No punch line, Jimbo. Unless watching her blow is your idea of a joke."

"Are you sure it's not *somebody's* idea of a joke?"

"Dead sure," he said. "X-rays bear it out. The C-4 and the detonators both show up."

"How did she find out?"

"He told her. She made a visit to his office in Brentwood, a routine follow-up to check a recent nip-and-tuck. And he laid it on the line."

"What do you mean?"

"He said, 'I love you, and if I can't have you, I'll destroy you.' Or words to that effect. Told her if she didn't go along, he'd blow up her boobs."

"Jesus," I said. "Isn't she already married? Didn't she marry that skinny washed-up rock star?"

"Skinny, washed-up, pussy-whipped, and *rich,*" he said. "He's sweating blood in Malibu. He's willing to pay a fortune to anyone who can rescue his little sex kitten. And, in case you were wondering, his little sex kitten knows you saved *Sea Crew*. She thinks you can save her too."

"I'm not sure I want to."

Linkletter ignored that. "We've got her isolated in a gym at a school in Malibu. In case Herschman hits the button."

"So he's got her triggered to go off by remote."

"That's right."

"How close does he have to be?"

"That, my friend, we do not know."

"She's safe for the moment?"

"Don't know. From the x-ray it looks like there's also a tracking device. For all we know, he's right outside. He gave her a few hours to think it over."

"Do you have a plan?"

"You'll offer him Patti," he said. "And a book deal. An 'as-told-to' thing. You know, a chance to say his piece. Once he and Patti are safely out of the country."

"She's willing to go along with that?"

"Yep. I mean, she'll never get on a plane with the guy. But she's willing to pretend she's giving in to him. Then—"

"She's not a very good actress," I said.

"I know that," he said. "The whole fucking world knows that. Which means a lot of this is gonna fall on you."

I couldn't see how I'd be in that much danger—as long as I kept clear of Patti and her tits.

"What time is Herschman calling?" I asked.

"Three o'clock."

It was 1.

"I take it you want me in Malibu."

He gave me an address on Point Dume.

I hung up.

Steve said, "What the hell was that all about?"

I sketched it out briefly as I hurriedly finished my lunch.

"Holy shit," he said. "You want me to come with you?"

"No way. You're too touchy-feely. You might want to give her a big hug—right when her boobs blow."

I had no particularly negative feelings about Patti Grant—unlike Diane Rainey, whom I seriously loathed. Patti was someone I hadn't given much thought to—except to the extent that you couldn't escape her picture on magazines, TV, everywhere actually. But if I had any take on her at all, it was basically a kind of cheap pity—that here was this woman who'd turned herself into a plastic doll.

So it wasn't hard to feel for her when I arrived and saw her predicament.

There she was, in the center of a large empty gymnasium, in a little makeshift area they'd set up for her. She was curled up on a sofa that looked as if it had been borrowed from a vice principal's office, next to a cot of the sort they provide for disaster evacuees. And beneath the cot was a hospital bedpan. She also had a table with a telephone and a small TV tuned to a soap opera. The picture, I could see even from my far-away vantage point, was fuzzy. No cable. She was dressed in shorts and a skimpy top that held her large, unnaturally round, potentially lethal breasts. Glassy, zonked eyes marred her airbrush-perfect features.

"What the hell is she on?" I asked.

"I gave her some Valium," said one of the suits, a tan guy

with silver hair. "I'm her regular physician."

"I need to talk to her."

Linkletter punched in her number, and I watched her sloppily pick up the receiver. "What?" she slurred.

"Patti, this is James Baker. The police and your husband have called me here to help."

It took her too long to put this together. "Oh. Oh, right." Her tongue was thick. "You're the guy who saved the cast from that thyco."

"Yes, that's me. Now listen, Patti. Herschman's going to call in a little while, and it's important that you do exactly as I say."

"Uh...uh..." She dropped the phone. Then she almost fell off the sofa as she picked it up. "What?" she said. "Could you repeat that?"

I covered the mouthpiece and turned to her doctor. "You gave her too much Valium. She's about to nod out. You've got to give her some speed or something. She has to be coherent by the time Herschman calls."

"I can order some Dexadrine from the pharmacy," he said.

"Do it. Now. We've got less than 90 minutes."

It was then, while the doctor used another phone to call the pharmacy, that Patti's husband, Derrick Crowley, arrived—drunk and frantic—with a teddy bear. "I'm back," he announced, grabbing the phone from me. Holding up the bear, he said to his wife, "Patti, I found it! I got Boopie for you, love! Hold on, love, and I'll bring him out to you."

Derrick started to open the door, but one of the cops stopped him. "Sir, for your own safety—"

"Fuck that," Derrick said. "Get out of my way! I'm not

afraid. I am going to take this bear to the woman I love!"

Now two cops stopped him. "Mr. Crowley, I'm sorry, but it's policy. For everyone's protection, including yours."

"I don't want to be protected," Derrick wailed. "I love her. Don't you understand? I've been with more birds than you'll ever count in the sky, but she's the only one I've ever loved. If she's going to die, let me die with her."

"That's very noble," one of the cops said. "But it's not going to happen. We can, however, send the bear out to her."

Derrick relinquished the stuffed toy, and the cops sent it out to Patti on a small furniture-moving pallet mounted on casters. They gave the pallet a good push across the gym floor, and she stumbled over to stop it. With the teddy bear clutched to her C-4 charged bosom, she blew Derrick a kiss, then slurred "Thank you" over the phone.

That's when one of the cops introduced me to Derrick. I was somewhat shocked by how messed up he was. I hadn't seen him in the media in a while, and he hadn't looked that great then. Now he was heroin-addict thin, with long, stringy, dirty, dyed-blond hair, bright, expensive, smelly clothes, and enough gin on his breath to start a fire if I'd struck a match. I mean, he made Keith Richards look healthy. He looked and smelled like a very tall, very thin, rotting dill pickle spear. His drunkenness didn't surprise me, though. He'd nearly died of alcohol poisoning during the last Satan's Stew tour, causing its abrupt cancellation. Back in '95, I think. He'd been in and out of rehab ever since. It was while he was out the last time that'd he met and eloped with Patti.

It was hard not to recoil from his breath and body stench

when he hugged me and said, "Thank God you're here! I know how you bailed out those *Sea Crew* kids. If you can save my Patti, I'll do anything. I'll pay you! A million dollars! And if you want a record deal—"

"That's all right," I said, and backed away from his odor as tactfully as I could. "I don't need a record deal, Derrick. But the money would come in handy."

"It's yours. If you save her from this psychopath, it's yours! A *million dollars!* I'm dead serious. If I go back on my word, feel free to call the tabloids and tell them I'm a scumbag. But I won't! A million dollars! If you can save my Patti, I will instruct my business manager to immediately cut you a check."

"Look," I told Derrick, "we've got a plan. But right now we're waiting for some speed to arrive. We can't proceed until it does."

Derrick got a stealthy look and I read his mind.

"You wouldn't be able to help out with that, would you?" I said.

Derrick and I looked at the cops in the room. They were looking back at us. Finally, Linkletter said, "Given the circumstances, we won't bust you. You have my word."

Derrick looked at me, and I nodded.

"All right," he said. "I shall return straight away."

Derrick came back in a minute from his car with a bag of crystal.

We sent it out to Patti on the cart, and Derrick gave her instructions over the phone on how much of it to snort. This was far better, of course, than waiting for the legal Dexedrine, which would have been in tablet form, thereby taking another 20 minutes or so to kick in. The effect of the crystal was virtually immediate.

It was almost comical to watch Patti's transformation from floppy rag doll to cranked-up replicant. "Come on, come on, talk," she snapped at me on the phone.

I filled her in on Linkletter's plan: that she'd talk Herschman into taking me along, and as soon as I saw an opening, I'd grab him and she'd grab the detonator. "You got it?" I said.

"Yeah, yeah, yeah, no sweat. I'm psyched now. We'll handle this fucker."

She was tweaked. Maybe too tweaked. But that was better than being nearly comatose. And the amphetamine omnipotence had the added virtue of overriding whatever terror she might otherwise have felt.

Still, all I could think about was blood, guts, and plastic on the bleachers.

Herschman called at 3 on the nose. As instructed, Patti let the phone ring three times. The cops, of course, had made arrangements for a trace. After the third ring, she picked up. Along with several of the police, I was listening on my own separate line. The only difference: Theirs were just earphones, whereas mine had a mouthpiece so I could chime in if and when I felt the time was right.

Patti said, "Hello?"

"Hey, pussycat." Herschman's tone was casual and intimate—creepy. "How are you doing?"

"Well," she said breathily, her version of Marilyn Monroe. "I don't really like what's going on, Donald. I mean, how would you feel if someone put bombs in your testicles?"

We'd decided to use this as the opener, to make him feel a little of what she was feeling. It worked.

"Eek!" he said. "I don't think I'd like that."

"Well, I didn't mean to upset you, Donald. But that's how I feel."

"Honeybunch, I know," he said. "And believe me, nobody's more sorry than me that it had to come to this. If you hadn't rejected me, this never would have happened. You'd never have known."

"I didn't reject you, Donald. At least I didn't mean to. I'm sorry if you took it that way." I'd coached her on that.

"I put my heart on your front porch. And you stepped on it, peaches."

"I didn't mean to step on it, Donald. Maybe I just didn't expect your heart to be there. I don't always watch where I'm walking. That's why I'm always stepping in...I mean...maybe it was, you know, dark out and I just didn't see it. You know?"

She was certainly a dim bulb. But at the same time she was perfect. If she hadn't bumped around like a blind poodle, she'd have sounded as if she was acting. In other words, wooden and unbelievable.

Pause. "What are you saying, Patti?"

"Just that...I guess you scared me, Donald. I mean, you startled me when you made, you know, your overture. You'd always been my doctor and one of my dearest friends. I guess I just...never allowed myself to think that maybe you felt for me the same way that...well, that I secretly felt for you."

Long pause. Derrick was listening too, and he began to sputter angrily. I made sure my mouthpiece was well covered.

Finally, Herschman said, "This smells like a trick."

"It's not," I said.

"Who the fuck are you?"

Patti answered for me. "His name is James Robert Baker. And I trust him. He's the writer that saved the *Sea Crew* cast. I told you about that, remember?"

It freaked me out that she'd confided in Herschman with something that big and that secret. Linkletter picked up on this vibe too, I could tell.

"Donald," she said, "this isn't a trick. I'm being straight with you. James is here with a business proposal. To write a book about us. So the world can hear *our* side of the story."

"I wish I could believe you, Patti," Herschman said. "You have to know you're telling me exactly what I want to hear."

"I know, Donald. But it happens to be the truth. I mean, I've always found you attractive, as many women do. But then...I *thought* I was in love with Derrick."

"That toad," the doctor said. "Worthless piece of shit."

I glanced at Derrick. Imploding. Still, the doctor wasn't wrong in his assessment.

"I was doing drugs when I met Derrick," Patti said. "I told you that."

More boundary-crossing intimacy. I looked at Linkletter, and I think we both sensed we were losing her, that she was falling for her own line of shit.

"Now that I'm clean and sober," she said, "it's like you go home with someone you meet while you're high at a club, and you think he's a prince. Then you wake up the next day and see he's a frog. Except it took me almost a year to wake up with Derrick."

This was not in the script.

Derrick was apoplectic.

I tried to step in for the save. "This is the sort of thing that would make for a good book, Dr. Herschman. This is what—"

"Shut up!" screamed Patti. "Shut up, shut up, shut up!"

Dead silence.

"Don't listen to anything he says, Donald. It's a trap. They were going to use him to kill you."

More silence.

"Donald," she said, "do you have your car with you?"

Linkletter buried his face in his hands. I shook my head in disgust.

"Donald," she said, "I'm coming out. If you don't see me outside in three minutes, I want you to blow me up. If anyone shoots at you, I want you to blow me up. And if anyone tries to follow us, a car or a helicopter or anything, I want you to blow me up."

"Pussycat, do you really mean it?" he said.

"I love you, Donald. I've loved you since I first met you. And I know now that you must love me too. You must love me desperately."

Then she said, "Donald, I love that you put bombs in my breasts."

To make a long story short, Patti and Mr. Hyde disappeared in his Porsche, Derrick went ape, and I didn't get paid.

Ⓐ

When I got back to the Vault, before I could even tell Steve what had happened, my cell phone rang. I recognized Dwayne's number and held up a finger, indicating to Steve that the call, at that time, was paramount.

"Hey, Dwayne. So?"

"Well, they're basically a rudimentary form of amphetamine," he said. "What was known in the '40s by its brand name, Benzedrine."

"Anything else?"

"Methobromate. What they used to call Miltown. A tranquilizer. Precursor to the benzos, like Valium and Xanax."

"I remember Miltown. Mom used to take it."

"So essentially it's like Dexamyl. Remember those?"

"Yep. Mom took those too. Upper cut with a downer to take off the edge. Anything else?"

"Yes, one more thing. And this one's the shocker. Asbestos."

"Asbestos?"

"That's what I said. Don't ask me how it worked or even *if* it worked. It is a fiber, though. It might have had a laxative effect. Or there could have been a metabolic interaction."

"So it *could* have worked as a weight-loss drug?"

"I suppose. But the long-term effects would be—"

"Cancer," I said.

"Precisely. Stomach, intestinal, bowel cancer."

"So it would be a tough sell to the FDA."

He laughed. "That's a safe bet. I hope nobody's still taking this crap."

"No. I think the last person who took it passed away very suddenly in 1945."

"Just as well. Otherwise the '70s might have held a grim surprise."

I thanked him and said I'd pick up the remaining pills—he'd only used three for his analysis—within a few days. Then I hung up.

Steve stared at me. "I don't even know what I should ask about first."

I gave him abbreviated versions of both the Patti Grant fiasco and the pill analysis, promising to fill him in later on the details. And then I called Diane Rainey.

"Hi," I said cheerily. "I got my results."

"So did we." Her tone was flat. Angry.

"And...?"

"I'm *very* disappointed. And *that* is putting it mildly."

"You realize they can't be used," I said. "Even if they work."

"I am aware that they are *not* what you promised."

"Excuse me?"

"I paid you to bring me a sample we could analyze. Not a worthless little nugget of chalk."

I smelled a dead rat. "Diane," I said, "I had no problem at all getting mine analyzed. Which lab did you take yours to?"

"That's none of your business. The point is, the pills were too degraded for the chemist to determine anything. By all rights, I should ask for my initial payment back. But I won't. However, I consider any further tentative arrangements with you null and void."

"Listen, bitch, you owe me money!" Not that I expected to get it.

"I don't think so," she said.

"The pills contain—"

She hung up.

I called her back and got her voice mail. I yelled the following message: "Asbestos, Diane! The pills contain *asbestos*! If you try to do anything with this junk, I'll have the FDA and the FBI on your fat right-wing ass so fast it'll make your triple chins spin. Got it, babe? " Click.

A minute later she called back. "You don't want to fuck with me, buddy boy."

"Don't threaten me, you fat sack of shit."

"If you fuck with me, you will get fucked back in a way that nobody wants to be fucked. Not even you, you faggot!" She practically spat the last word, then said, "Do I make myself clear?"

"No," I said. "I don't understand a fucking word you're saying, you fucked-up fuck hole. Eat my fuck!" Click.

Apparently, hanging around Vlad had influenced my vocabulary.

As we sat on the bed, Steve braced himself and made the crucial call to Tennessee. Naturally, it would have been much easier for Steve himself to return to Genesis as expected, for him to gather the evidence needed to prove they were making these bogus tapes. But he desperately didn't want to go back, and, frankly, I was afraid of what might happen if he did. He could flip back to Jesus and I would lose a guy I was starting to think of as my new boyfriend, not to mention my chance to nail a bunch of Christian scumbag fanatics.

"Hello, Ray?...Yeah, it's me...I sound funny? No, I'm fine. Really...Much better. My mom is doing much, much better. Praise the Lord."

It became clear that Ray had been trying to reach Steve at his old apartment. Steve explained his absence. "I had to leave that place. To get away from my addict friends. They were hounding me. I've been staying with a fine fellow. His name is Bill."

William Douglas was the name on the fake passport, California driver's license, and Adobe Corp. photo ID I'd be using.

Steve continued, "I met him at the church in Agoura. The one you told me about. He's a former alcoholic who used to beat his wife. Until he found the Lord last year. He's also a very gifted graphic artist. He used to design Satanic rock-album covers. And he knows computers. Before he found Jesus, he was doing postproduction work on music videos."

I was posing as an L.A.-based visual artist, hired by Adobe to home-test its software products. So I had to know something, I had to have used the products, but I didn't need to be a total expert. Steve and I both felt that given the limitations of a crash course, the role of technowizard would be hard to pull off. Especially since, if things went as planned, I'd be working with a guy who really was one.

"I've seen his work," Steve said. "It's very good. Although it's not the kind of thing he'd ever do again in terms of subject matter. And Ray, the thing is, I need to stay here a while longer with my mother."

Steve's cover story for leaving Genesis in the first place was that his mother had lung cancer and was undergoing surgery.

"Listen, Ray. I've told Bill a little about what we've been doing, and he's more than willing to fill in for me. We've even done a little work here. We made a picture of Tim Robbins having sex with Elton John."

In fact, we *had* done this, as a practical exercise during my crash course.

"It's good enough to sell to the tabloids. Although it needs some—"

Steve abruptly went silent, then handed me the phone.

Ray got right to the point. "So," he said in a gruff voice that made him sound like a guy in his late 50s, "I guess Stevie sort of spilled the beans." He forced a laugh. I could tell he wasn't pleased.

"He gave me a general sense of what you're doing," I said calmly.

"And how do you feel about it? Morally, I mean."

I thought for a second, and said, "The way I see it, there are two kinds of fighters. Those who fight dirty. And losers."

"Humph," he said. "Put Steve back on."

I handed the phone back to Steve. He listened for a moment, then said, "Ray, he's fine. And he picks things up quickly. I've been giving him some pointers, some of the stuff I learned from you. He's gotten *extremely* good with movement. He has a very deft hand." I smirked at that, squeezing his thigh.

After a moment, Steve handed me the phone again.

"All right, we'll see what you can do," Ray said. "Fact is, we have several crucial projects and Stevie's absence has put us way behind."

We made arrangements for me to fly out the next day.

Ray picked me up at the Nashville airport. He was what I expected. Close to 60, a grizzled porker with a creepy shag haircut. He gave me a hard handshake in the terminal, but his squinty eyes were filled with suspicion.

Driving to the Genesis compound on the outskirts of Nashville, Ray peppered me with questions. Personal stuff: What happened to my wife? How did I find Jesus?

I was prepared.

"We were living in Los Feliz, a section of Los Angeles," I told him, "when I woke up with the world's worst hangover. I could see right away that Sheila was gone." (My fake wives are always named Sheila.) "Her clothes were gone, everything. I guess I'd had a blackout the night before, because I have no memory of beating her up again. I got sick to my stomach, then turned on the TV. I flipped through the channels and came to Pat Robertson, who I usually laughed off. But he had a Word of Knowledge that was clearly about me. 'There's a man in Los Angeles,' he said, 'whose wife has just left him because of his drinking and violent behavior. And Jesus is entering his heart right now.'" I made my eyes well up with tears. "And it was true, Ray! I felt the Holy Ghost enter me. I felt the healing power of Christ, so I picked up the phone and spoke to a *700 Club* counselor. We prayed together and I was reborn. That was 14 months ago, and I haven't touched a drop of alcohol since."

"Praise Jesus," he said, and I knew I had him. "That was my problem too, Bill." He paused to choose his words. "I talk about this freely now because I know I've been forgiven. But sometimes the truth has to hit you in the face. Sometimes your head has to go through the windshield. That's what happened to me. I was drunk and hit another car. And crippled a sweet little girl."

I was startled and oddly moved—even though I knew he was still a scumbag—when I saw a tear roll down his cheek.

"I wanted to die after that," he said. "When I saw what Satan had caused me to do to that pretty little picture of innocence. But thank God my wife, may she rest in peace, brought me to Jesus."

"I'm sorry to hear about your wife," I said.

"So was I. But I'm not sorry about what happened to her killer."

"Her killer?"

"She was raped and murdered in Memphis. Four years ago. The cops blew the guy's head off when he wouldn't surrender," he said. "DeAnne was a saint. If that bastard had a grave, I'd take a shit on his headstone."

The compound was gated, set far back from the road, and surrounded by trees. Not visible at all to passing traffic. The main cluster of buildings was done in fake Regency style, at odds with the Greco-Roman fountain, antebellum gazebo, and Tudor garage—all foreshadowing the avalanche of kitsch to come.

Ray parked his Jeep Cherokee between a new Lexus and that quintessence of bad taste, a gold Rolls-Royce. As we climbed out, I had a major shock: A guy in his late 20s opened the front door of the main building and stepped out to greet us. Not bad-looking at all and with a nice body, which I could see very clearly since he was stark naked except for a pair of white socks and Nike shoes.

"Hi, I'm Joe," he said, extending his hand and smiling broadly with a telltale zealot's gleam in his eye. "Welcome to Genesis, Mr. Douglas."

I made no effort to hide my shock.

Ray saw my expression and laughed heartily. "Oh, Lord, that's right. You wouldn't know. I guess *Steve* doesn't know."

"Know what?"

We stepped into the foyer, and the receptionist, a middle-aged woman with big silver hair—there would be lots of big hair—was taking calls at the front desk with her baggy breasts exposed.

"Michael had a Word of Knowledge about a month ago," Ray said.

Steve had told me that Michael Collings was the head guy—a "reverend," who'd gone born-again in prison.

"The Lord instructed Michael that we should be as Eden. Before Eve bit the apple, she and Adam had no shame."

"I see." I wished I didn't.

"When the Lord speaks to him, Michael listens. And when Michael speaks to us, we know we're hearing the Word as he heard it from God. There's a changing room up here on the right. You'd best leave on your socks and shoes."

I watched a buck-naked tubby guy stroll down a hallway. I know you won't want to picture this, but he looked *a lot* like Rush Limbaugh.

I stepped into the changing room, where Ray and I both undressed.

"I can tell you're nervous," he said.

"To be honest, I had no idea..."

"That's all right. Most of us, like most decent people, were uneasy at first. There's so much association between nekkidness and sex. But it's a measure of our purity that here, in our own world, we can be as God's first kids."

"Makes sense, I guess."

As he pulled down his red bikini briefs, an uncut turkey-neck schlong flopped out. I saw him check out my cock too as I pulled off my flannel boxers. But it was blunt curiosity. I didn't catch any sort of gay vibe, repressed or otherwise.

"It's almost time for dinner," he said. "We all eat together in the main hall. Might as well head over there now. I know Michael is eager to meet you."

We started up an ugly green-carpeted hallway. The temperature was turned up high, higher than needed. I began to feel a bit claustrophobic and oddly disembodied. The last time I'd experienced anything like this was not gym class, where the naked trot to the showers was short, or even gay bathhouse visits, where most guys were wrapped in towels. It was my draft board medical exam. I hadn't been wearing any underwear, so they'd made me walk around naked.

The dining hall scene was gruesome. I'm trying to resist

trashing these people just because of the way they looked undressed. And to be honest, a few of the 100 or so present, like Joe, who'd greeted us at the front door, were OK. But most looked like overstuffed Jimmy Dean sausages. In short, pork city.

Ray was still introducing me around when Michael came in. From the way people reacted, you could tell right away that he was the big guy. Actually, though, he wasn't that big—in any department. About 5 foot 9, and in the dick division what I'd call average. In his late 50s, he had swept-back silver hair and snidely handsome features. According to Steve, he'd come from a wealthy New England family. He'd gone to Yale, then lived a fast-track life in Manhattan until his cocaine abuse led him to a crisis resolved by prison and the Lord. For a time he'd worked with Pat Robertson at CBN. Then he founded Genesis, which, when it wasn't fabricating videotapes, churned out vapid Christian television.

"Welcome," Michael said with a limp handshake. "We've been looking forward to your arrival. If you're half as talented as Steve, I'm sure you'll be a serious asset in our battle against the forces of Godlessness and depravity."

"I'm looking forward to it," I said.

"I must say, for someone from Southern California, you don't appear to be very fond of the sun."

"I burn easily," I said. Which is true.

"You seem familiar," he said. "Have we crossed paths?"

"I don't think so."

"Have you ever lived in New York?"

"No. But I go there quite a bit. Or used to. I have friends there. Or did. Struggling artists, no one you'd know. No one

I want to know anymore, if you know what I mean."

He smiled. "I do."

While we talked, I noticed that the two young men flanking Michael, who appeared to be his assistants, were by far the cutest of the men I'd seen since my arrival. Neither was effeminate. But one I caught glancing a shade too long at my cock. Suddenly my gaydar was picking up three fellow fags.

"I *know* I've seen you," Michael said. "If not in the flesh, then in the media. I never forget a face."

"Well, I've been in a few art magazines. Nothing tremendous. But they did use my photo."

"Ah," he said. "That must be it then. I once followed all of that quite avidly."

I thought the subject was closed, until he said, "But for some reason, I was thinking *writer.*"

"No. That wouldn't be me. I've never written anything. I was interviewed a few times. I was written *about.* Maybe that's what you're thinking of."

"You may be right. It's just that...I was connecting you with a *book* for some reason."

This was not good, though I thought I'd be all right. In any photo taken of me in the previous 10 years, I'd had a goatee or a full beard, and for this excursion I was clean-shaven. He'd have to go back to my first novel, *Adrenaline,* to find a photo of me they way I looked now. If that's what he was thinking of, his memory had to be sketchy. And presumably he didn't have a copy lying around. It's not what you'd call Christian reading.

I presumed wrong—as I found out after dinner.

Dinner itself was extremely successful. Ray and I shared

Michael's table, along with his docile, boyish assistants. Michael and I talked technology and politics. When it came to discussing the fake tapes, though, he went cryptic. It seemed clear this was a top-secret operation that Michael didn't want to broadcast to anyone at the other tables.

After dinner, Ray was leading me through a series of corridors to my room when we passed a small library, from which a bald-headed blob stepped out and said, "Hey, Ray. Take a look at this."

He had a porno magazine featuring a photo of a woman squatting over a man with the title: *Shit Happens.*

"Good Lord, Gene," Ray said. "I just ate."

"And guess where we found this. In a sex shop in Raleigh, N.C. Within two blocks of a high school and *one* block from a *church*!"

"This is just plain sick," Ray said. "Will you look at this, Bill?"

"I can't," I said. This was not an act. I have a problem with scat. I wouldn't ban it or anything. I mean, whatever. But it does turn my stomach.

"We notified the local D.A.," said Gene, "who, thank the Lord, is a Christian. They've shut the place down and arrested the owner. I figured this was one for the archives, all right."

"That's what this is?" I said as I stepped into the library.

"Yes, sir," said Gene. "So when the liberals talk about 'art' and 'freedom of speech,' we've got evidence of the kind of filth they really mean."

The collection, as you might expect, was inanely eclectic. They had hard-core pornography, both straight and gay, with an emphasis on fetishes, as well as shelves of serious literary fiction, including Alice Walker, Maya Angelou, and

The Catcher in the Rye. The collection was well organized, and I knew what I was looking for. I quickly spotted the black spine of *Adrenaline* and, while Gene and Ray were still occupied by the scat picture, slid it behind the wooden bookcase.

"Bill?" Ray looked over just a second after I hid my novel.

"I...I'm just...sickened," I said. I indicated a gay porno mag that featured a black guy cornholing a blond kid. "I can't believe our country's come to this, where it's OK to sell this kind of garbage."

"Well, it *has* come to this," Ray said. "But things are gonna change." He looked at the shelves, which held some of the best fiction of the 20th century. "Those who spewed this trash shall be held accountable. And not just in the next life. In this one too."

"As well they should," I said.

Ray slid his hand across my shoulder. "Come along, Bill. There's only one antidote for this kind of thing. There's no chapel tonight, but before you turn in, I believe we should spend some time with the Scriptures."

"Sounds good to me," I said. "I feel like I need a bath after that."

"Together," he said, "we shall bathe in the blood of the Lamb."

I was only half sure he was speaking figuratively.

In the morning, Ray woke me with a hand on my leg through the blanket. The blanket itself was what I'll call coagulated lamb's blood red, as was the wallpaper and the fabric of the white-and-gold-leaf French provincial furniture. They'd given me, by their standards, a *beautiful* room.

"Good news," Ray said. "You came back clean."

"Excuse me?"

"We ran a check. Standard procedure. To make sure you weren't some fed or reporter. But you're clean as a whistle. And we *are* thorough."

So was I. The party who'd supplied me with my new ID was a top-flight hacker. He'd dropped my new info into a number of databases, including those of law enforcement agencies and credit bureaus. I'd paid extra for that and was now glad I had.

Ray said, "Let's grab some grub and get to work, little buddy. We got a special visitor comin' today."

A note on this "little buddy" shtick: I wasn't really that much smaller, in any department, than Ray. But I do have a kind of boyish physique. And I think that our *nekkidness*—my younger body juxtaposed with his grizzled one—set off a protective older brother attitude on his part. Which, of course, I did everything I could to encourage.

"I'm all for that," I said, waiting for my morning erection to subside before I got up. "Let me shave and take a shower and...jeez, I almost said 'pull on some clothes.' "

After a greasy breakfast, Ray led me to the video suite, which was plush and state-of-the-art. "I brought you in here now, when we could be alone," he said, "because what I'm about to show you is beyond top secret." He booted up the system. "I've been working on this baby almost three years now. There's nothing like it on God's green earth. If I were so disposed, I could make a fortune off this. But the Lord has given me this wisdom not to make a billion dollars, but to wage a holy war against his foes." He looked at me, and said with gravity, "I call this the Revelations program." He clicked on a gold cross icon with the cute name "Nigvid," and said, "This is just a small sample of what it can do."

I silently watched, yet again, the O.J. murder tape.

"Jeepers," I said. "I can't believe how real it looks. I mean, I think that's exactly how it happened."

"It is. I assure you our research was flawless."

Well, not really.

I said, "I've seen good work before, but this...the faces."

"Yep. Faces are a tough nut. Unless you've got lots to work with. With these folks there was no lack of that."

"I take it you haven't used this yet. Or I'd know about it."

"Well..." Ray scowled. "That's a whole other story. We had a deal set up with a neighbor to make it look like he shot it. But he turned out to be less than reliable. So this one looks like a write-off. But we've got some new stuff going on that's even better."

He closed the file, opened another. This one named "Bitchvid." Not subtle. "Here's the one Steve was working on. I'll show you where we hit a snag."

The tape itself was in smeary black-and-white—simulated surveillance tape. The first few minutes showed Hillary Clinton and the late Vincent Foster having sex in an upscale hotel room. It began with her sucking his cock. Then he positioned her on the bed and let her have it from behind, doggy-style.

Technically it was good. The faces were theirs, absolutely

theirs, and the morphing of their changing facial expressions was, at least in real-time playback, flawless.

"How long did it take to do this?"

Ray shrugged, nonchalant. "Steve whipped this out in a couple of days. Of course, we were prepared. We already had the sex act. For that we used our own people. Now that's something you need to be aware of. It's tempting to use preexisting porno and just lay in new heads. But you'd be surprised how well sex addicts know this stuff—the same way queers know show tunes. And we don't want something coming back to haunt us, if you get what I mean."

"So you taped a couple *here*?"

Ray chuckled. "No way. We've got some couples here who would no doubt do anything Michael asked, but it was better and safer to hire a pair of scumbags with the right body types. And then take care of 'em once it was over."

I had a good idea what he meant by "take care of."

"Even then we had to tweak her legs," Ray said. "The tits were OK. But we had to thicken her calves and ankles. You know how she looks."

The picture cut to a new sequence, shot in similar black-and-white surveillance mode. The camera appeared to be hidden in what I took to be Foster's well-appointed office. He and Hillary were arguing, although there wasn't any sound. Then, in a scene reminiscent of a '40s film noir, she abruptly took a gun from her bag and shot Foster in the face. His back was to the camera, so you couldn't see the bullet hit him. But when he turned, as if he were trying to get away from Hillary, blood poured from his mouth. He hit the floor, and Hillary coldly stepped over him, picked up the phone on his desk, and punched a number.

"Of course," said Ray, "the way it is now, a crucial piece is missing. He was shot in the mouth all right. But the slug blew his brains out."

I saw where Ray was going, and I knew I had to deflect him. Even with Steve's crash course, I didn't have the skill to create a convincing exploding skull. Casually I said, "You know, it's interesting. I read a book a while back about this case. I forget the title. *The Foster Cover-up* or something like that. And according to the author, the autopsy mentions no exit wound at all."

Ray scowled. "That's hard to swallow. If the slug was a 38."

"Apparently there's some doubt about that," I said. "As you know, the bullet was never recovered."

To be honest, I didn't know if this was true or not. But I did know that if I were forced to create something that complex, I'd be quickly exposed as a fraud.

"Well," said Ray. "You'll have to talk to Michael. I'm sure he'll want to see this book."

"Sure. I think I still have it in L.A.," I said. "Can I take another look at the gunshot?"

I watched the replay several times. Then I said, "Yeah. I think if Foster just bleeds from his mouth, and Hillary coldly steps over him, that says everything we need to say. If we make it too messy, we'll just gross people out."

"Well, like I say, you'll have to talk to Michael."

"I will. I want to get this exactly right."

We heard the doors opening. Ray got up. "This could be your chance."

It was Michael, but he wasn't alone. He'd brought the visitor Ray had mentioned. In accordance with Genesis custom, he was naked except for his black socks and dress shoes. His 35-year-old body was pale and thin. His chest was hairless, but not his legs and butt. Below his dark brown pubic hair, his penis was what you'd have to call small. And his dweeby, boyish face was unmistakable, familiar from dozens of photos and TV interviews. The cunning and feared director of the powerful Christian Family Alliance looked at me and smiled, his eyes flitting over my cock, as Michael said, "Bill, I'd like you to meet Ed Keck."

I shook Ed's moist hand and said, "Praise the Lord. This is truly a shock and a pleasure."

"It's good to meet you, Bill," Ed said. "Michael tells me you're going to be filling in for Steven on some work we're doing."

"Well, yes." I wasn't acting nervous, I *was* nervous. Steve had never mentioned Ed Keck, or working with him, which was hard to understand. The CFA was growing more powerful by the day, and Keck, with his affable demeanor, was fast becoming the Christian Right's new media darling. "You know, I don't think Steven ever mentioned working with you, Ed."

Ed smiled, but his eyes were sneaky. "Well, we never really got around to working on that much." He held up a pair of videocassettes. "I did bring some material for a project he and I talked about, though."

For a second time, Ed's eyes swept my crotch.

"Let me show you what I've got," he said. "Just don't ask how I got it."

It was essentially a gay porno tape, albeit one shot surveillance-style, like the O.J. and Hillary tapes. The view was through a bedroom window, a Santa Fe style bedroom in which two men were going at it on a bed. One guy was in his late 20s, smooth and hairless, the other in his mid 30s, with an extremely hairy chest. It began pretty tamely, with mutual sucking on the Navajo bedspread.

"Speed it up," Michael said. "It gets worse."

Ray fast-forwarded through several minutes of sucking. Then the scene cut to a patio. A classic porn setting: swimming pool, palm trees, high fence. Although, again, it seemed unposed, taped spy camera-style through a crack in the wooden fence.

"OK, here," Ed said.

Back at normal speed, the smooth guy popped the lid from a can of Crisco and greased up his free hand and forearm. No surprise as to where things were headed. The lubed man formed a point with his sticky fingers, spread the legs of the hairy guy, and slowly started to fist-fuck him.

"So, what do you think?" Ed asked coolly.

"Well, the bodies are good," Ray said. "From what I've seen, they're a very good match."

"We certainly tried." Ed laughed. "Fortunately," and here he mentioned the name of an aggressively liberal, politically active, hairy-chested movie star, whom I'll call "Eric Perkins." "Fortunately, Perkins takes off his shirt in a lot of films. And we've got a number of butt shots as well. Same with," and here he mentioned a younger star, whom I'll call "Brian Stinson." Stinson has long been rumored to be gay. Perkins, however, has long been married to a Hollywood bombshell. His heterosexuality seemed beyond dispute—though clearly it wouldn't be if Genesis were to have its way.

"This is good," I said, trying to go along. "I think I saw a photo of Stinson in a magazine a while back. This really does look like his torso, as I recall it."

"Except he has a hernia scar now. Here." Ed pointed to his own groin. "There's a photo that shows it in last December's *Vanity Fair.* You'll want to put that in. The whole idea is that it has to look recent. Everybody knows Stinson is gay. It's an open secret. But we want it to look as if Perkins is not only gay but cheating on his gorgeous wife." Ed looked at me, his baby face hardening into a tight, mean mask. "We do *not* like Perkins. He's handsome, charismatic, and he has that knockout bitch wife. He could be a left-wing Ronald Reagan. That's what I see coming if we don't take him out now."

Michael smiled. "*Mrs.* Perkins is going to have a cow."

Ed put his hand on my shoulder. "Can you do it?"

"Sure. But I'll need some more material. More recent face stuff on both of them."

"There's no shortage of that. You can hit the local video store. And you might find *this* helpful." Ed handed me the second cassette he'd brought. The handwritten label read *Cease and Desist.* A legal thriller starring Eric Perkins. The last I'd heard it was still in production.

"Is that the finished film?" I said. "I thought they were still shooting."

"They are," Ed said. "These are the outtakes. Some *very telling* outtakes. There's a love scene between Eric and Sharon Beck. They're in bed together, naked, and the camera captures plenty of shots of his cock. At one point he does get aroused, so we've got a full Eric Perkins erection. Naturally, we want you to lay that in, so that even his wife says, 'My God, that's his cock!' You can do that, right?"

"Oh, yeah," I said. "With what Ray's just shown me, I can scan Eric's cock and re-create it from any angle."

Ed continued, "It's extremely important that we use his real cock. As you'll see, it's rather distinctive. Not enormous, except for the head. It has an extremely large head."

"How are things coming with the Stinson photos, Ed?" Michael asked.

"Not great." Ed turned to me and explained. "We heard an ex-boyfriend had some photos of Brian naked. But we can't track the guy down. You know how fags are. The guy could be dead."

"But we know Stinson is uncircumcised," Michael said with a creepy kind of Richard Nixon gravity. "And his cock size is average. But allegedly rather thick. So work with that for now."

"Will do."

The next morning, I woke up with Ed Keck in my room, on my bed, sucking my cock like a fiend. I didn't even know he'd spent the night at the compound.

My first reaction, as you might imagine, was heavy-duty shock, even though he'd set off my gaydar the day before. "My God," I said. "What are you doing?"

Ed stopped sucking long enough to say, "Just relax. It's OK. No one is going to know."

He went back to sucking. And he was good. But still vile.

Waking up fast, I tried to decide how to react. How, as a born-again Christian, I *should* react. I finally pushed him away, gently but firmly, and sat up, pulling the sheets up over my crotch. "Ed, no. This is wrong. You know this is wrong."

He was naked himself, of course, with a rock-hard erection.

"I wanna suck your cock," he said with glazed eyes. "I wanna suck the come right out of it."

Stroking himself with one hand, he tried to reach under the sheets to grab me again.

I brushed his hand away. "Ed, no, please. This is a sin."

He stared at me, still squeezing his erection. He looked mad, frustrated, disappointed, even hurt. But mostly mad. "Are you trying to tell me you never fooled around with Steven?"

This was not what I wanted to hear. "That's crazy. Steve and I are just friends. Christian brothers."

"Bullshit," he said. "Steven's never *just friends* with anybody." Again he tried to reach under the sheets.

"Ed, please. I respect you. I admire what you're doing. Especially your stand against gay rights. That's why I frankly do not understand this. I'm very confused."

After a long, scary pause he said, "Let me explain." And to my relief, he pulled the sheet up to cover his wilting erection. "This is my off-the-record belief. What you and I have just done will never be accepted by most people. Even liberals, who pretend to *like* gays, are secretly disgusted. And they always will be. That's human nature and you can't change that. The worst thing that ever happened to people like us was the so-called gay rights movement. For centuries, people like us lived comfortably in their closets until the left-wing radicals ripped all the doors off their hinges. The moment they did that, they sent their so-called brothers and sisters packing down the long and winding yellow brick road that leads not to Oz but to genocide."

"Genocide?"

"That *will* come. You'll see. It's inevitable. Clinton's America was the Weimar Republic. And you know what came after that. I'd never say this on C-SPAN," he said. "But I admire Hitler. In truth, as many secretly know though few will admit, he did the *right thing* with the Jews. And I will do the same with the militant homosexuals. And with anyone else who gets in my way. Once I'm elected president in 2008. Or 2012 at the latest."

This was crazy. This guy had just sucked on my cock. Now he was lauding Adolf Hitler and telling me that if he became president he would exterminate millions of gays.

"How are you going to do that, Ed? I mean, how are you going to run for president if you like to do what you just did?"

"Oh, I've got that covered. I'm going to get married next year. To a woman. That's all set up. As far as this sort of thing goes," he put his hand on my knee, "I'm *very* careful."

Right. Try very deluded. His behavior smacked of hard-core sexual compulsion. If he ever ran for office, guys would be crawling out of the woodwork to sell their stories to the tabloids.

"I'd like to see you again," he said. "Frankly, while I did enjoy Steven, you're much more my type. Although, I have to say, I don't like the one-way street thing. I expect—demand, really—complete reciprocation."

I imagined beating the shit out of Steve.

"I'm really confused," I said. "Because the Bible makes it clear—"

"Let me tell you a secret." He spoke softly and carefully. "Something that very few Christians know. The Bible is truly the word of God. But...it was written for the man in the street, at a time when people behaved like animals, when God knew that without a set of rules there would be anarchy. There has always been a select few for whom God has made a different, hidden set of rules. And they—we—answer directly to God. We are charged with a sometimes terrible mission. But along with this, there are perks. Do you understand what I'm telling you?"

"Yes. I mean, I think so."

He glanced at his wristwatch. "I can explain it more thoroughly later. Right now I have a meeting with Michael. I'm glad you're here, Bill. I'm glad we've met. I have a special feeling about you."

"I...I don't know what to say." And I really didn't.

"You don't have to say anything. I understand your confusion. Steven and others have felt much the same way. Initially. But trust me when I tell you I can show you the way." Ed got up, finally. "The official rules are still quite real. They are needed for the masses. But God is generous toward those of us chosen to do his special work. And I will tell you this: Michael is quite brilliant; he is also useful; but he is *not* among the chosen. So I will never speak to him of...this. Nor should you. Given his past, it would provoke great fury. Do you understand?"

"I think so."

Ed paused at the door to say, "I'm going to be here for several days. Michael and I have many things to speak of. I'm looking forward to seeing what you do with the tape. And I'm also looking forward to a great deal more of what we've just begun. I'll leave you with a final word to the wise..." He smiled serenely and whispered, "Reciprocate."

Then he was gone.

I spent the day working on the Perkins-Stinson tape with Ray because I couldn't afford to arouse suspicion. The outtakes from *Cease and Desist* contained everything Ed had mentioned, including the shot of Eric with a hard-on. You could hear the crew breaking up, and Eric was laughing too, to cover his embarrassment as he yelled at the cameraman, "Shut that fucking thing off! If this shows up on the Internet, I'll have your heads!"

We lifted his erection from the outtake, stuck it in the porno clip, and began making adjustments. Had we been working with a single photo, it would have taken several hours to get it right. With a moving image the process was much more involved. To get everything seamless would take, we'd guessed, at least a month.

Worse, I wasn't really up to the job. I made an early mistake with one of the tools, a basic erasure tool. "What are you *doing*?" Ray said as I accidentally wiped Perkins' balls off the screen.

"Sorry. I didn't really sleep well last night. I'm a little punchy, I guess."

He bought it, I think, though I did catch a flash of suspicion.

Ⓐ

Late in the day I told Ray that I wanted to go out and purchase some videos featuring Perkins and Stinson, and I drove into Nashville in a Genesis Acura to pick them up at a local video store. Once in town, when I was pretty sure I hadn't been followed, I used a pay phone to call Steve in L.A.

I'd decided not to mention the Ed Keck thing. I didn't want to confront him about that on the phone. I had another agenda. "Look. This isn't working," I told him. "I don't know enough, and Ray's suspicious. You've got to help me get out of here."

"Get you out? What's wrong? They haven't busted you, have they? What have they said about me? What's going on?"

He was motormouthed. He sounded paranoid.

He was tweaked.

"I just told you. We're working on a tape involving a movie star. Cutting his head and dick into a gay porno tape."

"His dick?"

"His penis. His cock. You know that thing guys have between their legs? And it's becoming apparent to Ray that I do *not* know what I'm doing. I mean, I know *some* stuff. But not enough. You've got to get me out before they realize I'm a fake. I need you to call with some sort of emergency."

"What do you mean? Right now?"

I heard a door close in the background on his side of the line. "Who's there?" I asked.

"Where?"

"*There*. In the house with you. I heard someone."

"That was me," he said. "It's getting cold. I just closed the patio door."

"Oh. So can you call Genesis in an hour? Tell them...I don't know. That you had appendicitis. That you're in the hospital."

"They could check that. And later, if I do come back, they'll expect to see a scar."

True. Especially since they'd gone nekkid.

"I've got it," I said. "Say you've had a relapse."

"Why should I say that?"

Because it's true, I thought. But I was saving that for later, too. "It's perfect," I said. "You can call and tell me, and Ray and Michael or whoever, that you had a one-night speed relapse. But now you're remorseful and going back to church. But you need my support as a close friend in Christ."

He thought about it a moment. "So you're aborting the whole mission? After all the stuff I taught you?"

"I'm not giving up. That's why I want to leave the door open. I have a better idea of what I need to know now, regarding this tape we're doing. Maybe if I have another few days of instruction... So can you do it?"

"Do what?"

Steve called that night shortly after I got back to the compound. He talked to me first, staying "in character" in case our call was monitored, and I used another line to call Michael. Michael punched the line Steve was on, and we both listened to his story of the one-night relapse. For whatever reason,

Steve was calmer now. I guessed that he'd taken some tranquilizers. Xanax or Valium or something. He sounded much saner than he had earlier. He sounded genuinely remorseful—maybe he was—and convincing.

"You need to come back, Steve," Michael told him gently. "I was afraid this might happen. L.A. is not a safe place for you."

Steve spoke of his mother's grim post-op condition. "She's still in pain all the time," he said. "The doctors aren't giving her enough medication. It's absurd. I can't leave until I get this straightened out."

Michael finally agreed to let me go back to watch over Steve. "But I want both of you to go to the church in Agoura as often as you can," he said. "I do *not* want to lose either of you."

I didn't sleep well that night. There was no lock on my door, and I was afraid Ed Keck would find out I was leaving in the morning and try to stick his cock in my mouth before I was gone. But the call from Steve had come late. Most likely, by the time Ed learned of my departure I was already eating breakfast on the plane back to L.A.

"You lied to me, Steve," I told him as we drove home from LAX.

He was at the wheel of the Land Cruiser. "What are you talking about? What did I lie to you about?"

"OK, maybe 'lie' is the wrong word. You left things out."

"What things?"

"The fact that you fucked Ed Keck."

To his credit, I suppose, he just said, "Oh, shit. How did you find out?"

"He told me. After he sucked my cock."

"*What?*"

I described what had happened. "Why didn't you tell me about Ed?"

"OK." He glanced at me apprehensively. "Real reason? Because he laid the same trip on *me.* That's the reason I had to get out of there too. Ed wanted me to come and live with him. To be his *boy* or whatever. He's insane."

"I know."

"What happened with me was very similar," Steve said. "He came into my room while he was visiting. And the next thing I knew he was rubbing my crotch through my pants. And I kind of went into shock. I mean, I couldn't believe what was happening. Since he's like the world's biggest homophobe."

"Well, it's a little different now. No rubbing through the pants. They've gone nude."

"*What?*"

I explained.

He was incredulous at first. Then he laughed. "That is too bizarre! Michael must be flipping out."

"Did you do it with Michael too?"

"No," he said adamantly. "Michael's a *cured* gay."

"Are you sure? He's got an entourage of cute guys."

"Yeah, I know." Steve shrugged. "He's still gay in his soul.

But he doesn't do anything anymore. I don't think. He never came on to *me*. But then I never let him know about that side of me. It was always just the drugs."

"Speaking of which...?"

He stared ahead at the freeway. "Yeah, OK. I scored an eight ball. I had the craving again, and without Jesus or Michael... I know I fucked up. I made a mistake. I take full responsibility." There were tears in his eyes. "I don't want to lose you, Jim."

"Did you fuck anybody else while I was gone?"

"*No*. And that's the truth."

I wanted to believe him. And something told me I could.

But something had shifted. A door had been closed. I still *cared* about Steve. But in my heart I was hearing "The Thrill Is Gone."

The next morning, shock of shocks, Diane Rainey called.

"What's on your mind, Diane?"

"First off, an apology." Her syrupy voice oozed fake good will. "I'm a bitch. I guess that's no secret. You did *not* deserve what I said to you. I have no explanation, except that it was already a bad day for me. If you get what I mean, without discussing the female issues."

"Sure. Whatever."

"And I was, of course, disappointed about the product initially."

"I'm not sure I understand," I told her.

"Well, first of all, let me say that I've learned a bit about what you went through to procure the product for me. In Germany especially. Don't ask me how I found out."

I could tell she was leery of saying too much on the phone. So was I.

"So what's this leading to?" I said.

"Well, with a better understanding now of what you endured, I do feel you earned the rest of your fee. And I'm prepared to pay you. And that's just for starters."

I was way ahead of her. But I said, "Let me be sure I'm clear. You're willing to pay me the second half of the initial fee we discussed?"

"Yes."

"When? How?"

"Today, if you'd like. You can come by the house, and I can call the bank. I'll have them make a transfer to your account. Then you can check it yourself to make sure it's there."

"Sounds good."

"Four o'clock?"

"Fine. I'll be there."

"Jim, I really am sorry for the awful things I said to you. I'd like us to be friends again. Do you think you can ever forgive me?"

"I'll work on it," I said. "See you at 4."

I hung up, knowing exactly what the sneaky cooze was up to. She was going to try to buy my silence so she could go ahead and make the pills.

Whatever she offered, I planned to agree. I might dicker first, to make it more convincing. And I'd do nothing until *after* she made the bank transfer. Then I'd find out as much as

I could about where she planned to have the pills manufactured. I might even wait until they'd cranked out their first batch and she had her own supply. Then I'd bust her fat ass with a hot tip to the FDA.

I left a few minutes before 4 o'clock with a Sony microcassette recorder hidden in my windbreaker pocket. It was a tricky move, since I'd be recording myself as well, and I planned to keep my tip to the FDA anonymous. But Diane was likely to say a lot that would incriminate *her,* in which case a recording might come in handy. An edited recording if she started blabbing about my European experiences. I'd have to see what I got.

When I reached Diane's, the front gate was open, which didn't especially alarm me. She was, after all, expecting me. I drove on in and parked in the driveway, which was empty. The front door of the house was open too. Now I was alarmed. I'd seen too many crime films with a similar scenario not to get a bad feeling.

I knocked on the open front door and called out, "Diane?"

No answer.

I stepped into the foyer, and that's where I caught my first whiff of a terrible odor. An oddly sweet stench—something burning, something left in the oven too long. Candied ham, maybe.

Then I heard the microwave humming.

It was a large and beautiful kitchen, with state-of-the-art

appliances: huge stove, subzero walk-in freezer, central counter and sink. The floor was a delicately patterned Spanish tile. The room was spotless. The only sign of disarray was a white plastic trash bag discarded on the floor below the microwave. The bag was smeared with wet blood.

The microwave was the kind with a glass carousel. Inside, Diane's severed head rotated slowly. Her skin was smoking and bubbling, her tongue had turned gray and plumped like a hot dog. As I watched, her left eyeball exploded.

Well, I've seen some bad shit, but nothing quite this bad. I knew I was going to be sick, so I rushed down the hall to the first bathroom, a guest bathroom, where I puked in the toilet. I was shaking as I got up, flushed the toilet, and splashed water on my face at the sink. I had the presence of mind, though, to use a hand towel as a makeshift glove so I wouldn't leave fingerprints.

My number 1 goal was to get the fuck out of there.

Then I heard someone else in the house. I froze in terror. I knew it was the Russians who'd done this to Diane, and my first thought was, *It's them. They're still here.*

But it was Biff. I heard his distinctive gruff voice call out, "Hey, Diane! I'm home! What the fuck is that smell?"

Before he could get to the kitchen, the phone rang. He stopped to answer it.

"Yeah, what?" he barked. "Yeah, yeah. I'm fine, Jorge. Look, here's the thing. You haven't made the labels, right?"

I took out my recorder and hit the red button.

"Good," Biff said. "Because we're changing the name. Evadrine's no good. Sounds too feminine. No, *feminine,* Jorge!" He was irritated and overenunciating, as if Jorge didn't speak English very well. "Evadrine makes it sound like a douche. We want to make it guy-friendly. Evadrine's too babe-like. We might as well call it Vaginadrine. *Vag—* Never mind."

Biff listened for a moment. "OK, Jorge, look! Write this down!" He was shouting, I realized, because Jorge was in Mexico, and they either had a crummy connection or, more likely, Biff was the kind of moron who thought you had to shout if the call was long distance. "Berchedrine!" he yelled. "No, *Berch-e-drine!"* He spelled it out, twice. "It works, Jorge! It still evokes the story of where it came from, but it's not so chick-like."

At this point I stepped out of the bathroom and made my way down the hall to where I could see Biff, with his back to me, in the living room. His buzz cut was died a bright punk green for the sci-fi film he was shooting. Once he was done with the call I knew he'd head for the kitchen. And that would be my chance to get the fuck out. Of course, he'd seen my car—or rather Phil's Land Cruiser—but I doubted that he'd paused to memorize the license number.

"Ingredients listing? Are you *crazy*? Are you *nuts*? Are you *loco*? *Comprende? Loco?"*

He listened for a moment. Then he said, "Of course we're going to tell people what's in the pills! These are going to our *friends,* Jorge! We're also going to tell them they fucking work! After that, it's their call."

He covered the mouthpiece and again called, "Diane?" Then he said to Jorge, "Look, I gotta go. But nothing on the label except the name, *comprende*?" And with that he hung up.

He headed straight for the kitchen. For a second there was

nothing. Then he howled. A torturous, seemingly endless howl. Diane was a fat mean bitch, but she had been his other half, after all.

Biff was still howling when I ducked out the front door, climbed into the Land Cruiser, and coasted down the driveway without starting the engine. Finally, as I rolled through the gate, I fired the ignition and sped away.

It occurred to me that Diane, in dying, had stiffed me yet again.

Needless to say, Diane's death was the lead story on the news that night.

The cops had made the Russian Mafia connection. After all, Diane's headless, bloated body had been dumped in the swimming pool, and she'd been decapitated with an electric knife, just as Ken had. A "trademark" was how one reporter put it. The police had no idea why the Russian Mafia might have had it in for Diane Rainey, and they were looking for an unidentified white Land Cruiser. The reporters were almost as interested in Diane's surprising girth as her decapitation. Nothing unexpected.

The shockers came later that night. I was channel-surfing through the local news programs, with Steve beside me on the bed, when I came to one showing a photo of Vlad. "Police are now seeking former Russian diplomat Vladimir Kandinsky, who was allegedly seen in Laguna Beach three days ago."

I pictured Vlad with the dime-size bullet hole in his forehead.

The prospect that Vlad might be alive, back in the United States, and that he might have been among those who'd killed Diane, was extremely unsettling. And even if Vlad was truly dead, the fact that his comrades had tracked me back to Diane was equally unsettling.

I stared at the cop-and-reporter-clogged crime scene on TV. "This is pretty over-the-top," I said.

"No shit," Steve said. "You missed a horrible tidbit, by the way, when you were taking a leak."

"What's that?"

"When they dragged her body from the pool, they found her stomach cut open. Like to search the contents, it sounded like."

We spent the next few days holed up at the Vault, fending off calls from both Michael and Ray. We worked hard on the computer stuff, and I began to feel more comfortable.

Steve, however, seemed to be getting *un*comfortable. No doubt in part because I begged off having sex. I'd said I thought I might be coming down with a cold. *Cold* was the right word, but it wasn't a virus. I was chilling on him, and he knew it.

"Do we have a problem?" he said, after he tried to hug me from behind as I sat at the computer and I involuntarily cringed.

"You just startled me, that's all."

"OK," he said. "Just checking."

"Everything's fine," I said. "I'm just a little charred. From trying to learn all this so quickly."

"Well, you need to know it," he said, "or they'll bust you when you go back."

"I'm aware of that."

He really was trying to help me. And I knew that he did care for me. So I felt kind of crummy that in my mind I'd already moved on.

Finally, I felt comfortable enough with the graphics program to go back to Genesis. And none too soon. Things with Steve and me were getting *very* strained.

Steve dropped me off at LAX in Phil's Jaguar. Getting ready to leave, he'd asked why we weren't taking the Land Cruiser.

"I don't want to be hassled," I'd said. "Everybody knows they're looking for a white Land Cruiser in connection with the Diane Rainey murder. And the Vault is only about five blocks away from her house. I don't want to be stopped. You shouldn't drive it either."

"Be careful," he said, as I got out at the airport. "Let me know what's up."

"I will. As soon as I can."

If I'd still been in love with him, I would have leaned into the Jag and kissed him.

Ⓐ

As soon as I saw Ray, I said, "My God. What's wrong?"

His skin was jaundiced and sweaty, his breathing labored. And he was dressed.

"Past catchin' up with me," he said. "Bum liver. Too much alcohol, too many drugs. I thought I was healed, but maybe you can only cross the Lord so many times. I don't like hospitals," he said, "but that's where I'm headed."

So that's why they'd been so desperate for Steve and/or me to come back.

"Think you can handle things?" he asked.

"Yeah, sure. Did we get anything on Stinson?"

Michael nodded. "Everything you'll need."

One of Michael's cute young assistants arrived. He was also dressed. To accompany Ray to the hospital, I presumed. "The ambulance is here."

I gave Ray a quick hug, and the assistant helped him out. As he left, I said, "May the Lord be with you, Ray."

"I believe in his will," Ray said. "My fate is in his hands." He forced a smile. "You do a good job, you hear? The future of our country depends on it."

"Don't worry. I won't let you down."

Once Ray was gone, Michael shook his head. "He's in bad shape. It's more than his liver. I'm not sure he's going to make it."

"Well," I said. "I guess I'd better get to work." More to get away from Michael than anything else.

Ⓐ

The next morning, ragged from lack of sleep—Ed Keck was long gone by this time, but I could still feel the shock of waking up to find the most notorious homophobe in America sucking my cock—I went jogging outside the compound, just so I could use the pay phone at a gas station down the road to call Steve. I needed to ask some technical questions, but before I could do that, Steve blurted, "The cops were here and I'm using again and Biff Decker tried to kill me."

"Whoa. Hold on," I said. "When did all this happen?"

"OK," he said, clearly tweaked. "First thing that happened, yesterday I go to the market. Chalet Gourmet. In the Land Cruiser, OK."

"Jesus, Steve! I told you not to drive the Land Cruiser!"

"I know. But this is what happens. I'm at Chalet Gourmet in the cheese aisle when Biff Decker, out of nowhere, grabs me from behind and tries to strangle me. Like in a total rage, red-faced, the whole bit. Screaming that I'm the one who killed his wife. 'You fucking piece of shit, you're gonna die right now!' I mean, he's choking me. It took the manager and two stock boys to pull him off. And of course the cops came. But get this. This is the weird part. He thinks I'm *you.*"

"What do you mean?" Like I didn't already know.

"He's calling me *Jimbo.* Like, 'Say good night, Jimbo,' while he's trying to strangle me. So when the cops arrive, it comes out that he saw me pull up to the market in the Land Cruiser, which is just like the one he says was at his house right before he found Diane. And he says he knows *you* drive one. That you were involved with Diane in some deal. That you got pissed off and killed her."

"What did the cops say?"

"They don't buy Biff's version. They think the Russian Mafia did it, just like they say on the news. They tried to chill Biff out, but he wouldn't chill. He still thinks you did it, for whatever reason." Steve hesitated. "Did you?"

I laughed. "I did not kill Diane Rainey." Sometimes telling the truth is very easy.

"Anyhow, the cops came to the house."

"The Vault?"

"Yeah. This was later, after I got home. It was actually just one cop, some guy who says you know him. Linkletter. From homicide."

This wasn't so bad. "What did he say?"

"That he wants to talk to you."

"You didn't tell him where I am, did you?"

"Of course not. I said I didn't know where you were. That you'd gone off on some gonzo adventure."

"Good."

"He did give you a message, though."

"Which is?"

"He doesn't think you did it. He doesn't think you killed Diane. But he thinks you were there. That maybe you walked in on the scene before Biff did."

"That's screwy," I said. "So when did you start using again?"

"Last night. I didn't intend to, honest. On the contrary. I was upset over the thing with Biff and the cops and all. So I did like they say and went to a meeting."

"A crystal meth meeting?"

"Yeah. And I *shared* and everything. But here's what happened. Right while I was sharing, this ex-boyfriend of mine, Kevin, a guy I used to do crystal with, comes in late. So at the break, we got to talking and one thing led to another..."

"So you went home with him."

"No. Look, I know this is going to piss you off, but I invited him up here. And he still had some crystal, so..."

"Is he still there?"

Long pause. "Yes."

I was boiling, but I kept an even tone. "Listen closely, Steve. I want you both out of the house, right now. Immediately. Pack your shit and get the fuck out. You've got 30 minutes. As soon as I hang up, I'm calling Westec. You hear what I'm saying? If you're still there in 30 minutes, you'll be arrested for trespassing. I can't have you tearing up the house when it's not even mine."

He started to say something, but I hung up. Then I called Westec security. "If they're still there when you go by, call the police."

When I got back to the compound, Michael was waiting for me in the video lab. His expression told me what he was going to say before he said it. "Ray...is with the Lord."

"Oh, no."

"It's a loss," Michael said. "But weep not for him. He is with his personal savior. He sits even now at the right hand of our Lord, Jesus Christ."

"I'm sure he does. Bless his everlasting soul. I'm...I don't know what to say."

"The best thing you could do, the greatest tribute to Ray, will be the continuation of his work. Are you up to that, Bill?"

"Absolutely," I said with resolve. I showed him the latest work.

"It looks good," he said. "But it has to be perfect. Absolutely flawless. This tape will be studied like nothing since the Zapruder film."

Since I was working alone in the lab now, I was free to turn my attention to my real mission: finding a way to copy the Revelations program, which was, in fact, a work of genius. Even though it technically plagiarized vast chunks of other visual-editing programs, it recombined and integrated the best features, along with its own unique ones, resulting in the ultimate video software program, far superior to anything else available. Its output, as the O.J. tape had proved, could be utterly convincing and undetectable. And, of course, if it could be used by right-wing extremists, it could also be used against them. So I wanted it.

But while I could access it on the hard drive, I couldn't make a duplicate. Ray had installed an elaborate copy guard. It came down to knowing a password. There was a copy option, if Ray had ever wanted to back up the program, but it was password protected. I played around with the password, trying obvious choices: *DeAnne* (his wife), *God, Jesus, Genesis, Adam, Eve,* even *Satan.* But I struck out.

The other approach was to look for a back door, which is essentially what it sounds like: an unprotected entrance into an otherwise secure program. The back door is usually, but not always, through one of the system files. I searched them methodically, since this was my best bet, but struck out there too.

Then, late the next night, while working in the lab, I got a phone call. "It's someone named Brian in Los Angeles," the male Genesis bot told me. "He says he's Steve's sponsor and needs to speak to you."

Well, I kind of shit, wondering how Steve's *sponsor,* which meant his 12-step mentor, had gotten this number. Or *not* wondering, actually. Steve had clearly told him where I was—and how much else?

My heart pounded as I took the call, not certain what this guy was going to say—with the bot, almost certainly, listening in.

"Hello?"

"Is this, uh, Bill?"

"Yes. Who is this?" Praise God for small miracles: At least he hadn't blown my cover. But he *knew about* my cover!

"This is Roger. I'm Steve's sponsor, or I was. In his, uh, recovery program."

Heart still pounding. "Yes?"

"I just thought you should know..." His voice had a subtly queeny tone. At least *I* picked up on it, but maybe the bot wouldn't, assuming he was monitoring the call. "I just thought I should let you know that Steve, since his recent slip, has reaffirmed his commitment to Christ. In the most profound way. Do you understand what I'm telling you?"

I did, bless his heart. He was *warning* me. Steve must've told him what I was up to, that I'd infiltrated Genesis, everything.

I played along. "That's good to hear, Brian. I take it you're calling from the, uh, church in Agoura."

"I'm calling from home. But Steve has moved into the Agoura compound. After all of his slips, he came to feel it was the only safe place to be. To be free from temptation, in a Christian setting. I just thought you'd like to know."

"I'm glad you called, Roger," I said, measuring my words. "I've been very concerned about Steven and his drug problem. It's good to know that he's made this decision."

"Yes, I felt that you'd want to know. I also know that he wants to go back to Genesis as soon as he's stabilized. And I believe he intends to call the head fellow, Michael, very soon."

"Michael Collings?"

"Yes, that's right."

"I see."

"I hope you do. I felt it was very important that you know about Steve's current situation."

"I appreciate your bringing it to my attention."

"Not at all. Steve has recommitted himself with great fervency and zeal to doing the Lord's work. And I wanted you to know he'll soon be doing everything he can to help...to help the cause."

"That's good to know," I said. "Thanks again, Roger. God bless."

"May God bless you too. In Jesus' name."

"Amen."

I hung up and sat for a moment, considering. Oddly, I felt a sudden sense of calm. My heart had stopped pounding. Brian's warning had been fairly ingenuous. He'd obviously known the call might be monitored, and he clearly knew the true nature of my business there. He'd managed to let me know that Steve had gone back to the fundies and would soon be calling Michael to blow the whistle on me—all without saying anything an eavesdropping bot was likely to decipher.

But how did I know that Steve hadn't already called Michael, or wouldn't, very soon?

It was time to leave.

I walked to a construction site in the compound, where I'd spotted an acetylene torch the previous day. It was still there. Relatively small, it fit easily into my satchel. No one saw me pick it up. At that hour the grounds were nearly deserted. Then I went back to the studio.

Once inside, I removed the hard drive containing the Revelations program. If I couldn't copy it, I could at least take it with me. I wasn't sure this would actually work, which is why I'd spent so much time trying to copy it. But given the circumstances, it was my only option.

The next step was easy. I fired up the torch and melted anything in the room that could possibly have held a copy of the program or clips—hard drives, Jazz disks, CD-ROMs, videotapes, everything.

The fumes were pretty bad, especially from the disks and videotapes. By the time I was done gutting the place, the room was thick with acrid smoke and I was struggling to breathe. I gave the room a final once-over to see if I'd missed anything. I hadn't. So I shut off the torch and left it on a half-melted keyboard.

I stepped from the studio, satchel in hand, closing the door on the smoke and the odor. I almost shit when I saw Michael walking toward me.

It was clear he hadn't talked to Steve yet, or he wouldn't have been alone. And he wouldn't have been smiling.

"You're working late," he said as he reached me.

"Well, yes," I said. "I'm into the tricky part now. And I want to get it right."

"Can I see how it's coming?"

I was ready for that, sort of. "Not right now. I just started a video rendering that's going to take several hours. It's set to shut off when it's done. In the morning we'll be able to see the results. I promise you're going to be impressed."

"I hope so." He was buying it. "By the way, I hate to lean on you, I can see that you're exhausted. But the sooner we get this, the better."

"That won't be a problem. But I can't rush. As you've said yourself, it has to be flawless."

"I trust your abilities, especially since I talked to Steve."

This shook me. "When did you talk to Steve?"

"Last weekend," he said. "Right before you came back. By the way, I've been trying to reach him at that number in L.A. No answer. Have you spoken with him since you've been back?"

Either he was testing me, or the call from Brian hadn't been monitored.

"Not directly. But I did get a call from a friend of his earlier this evening. He told me Steve was still having some temptation, so he moved into the Agoura compound. To be in a safe Christian atmosphere. I told him I thought it was a good idea, given Steve's unfortunate relapse history."

Michael shook his head. "Speed. A terrible drug. A demonic drug, quite literally. I'll call him in the morning. It's a bit late now." He considered. "Although it's only 10:30 Pacific time..."

"You might want to wait," I said. "Their policy is early to

bed, early to rise. I intend to call him myself in the morning."

"Yes. Perhaps we can call him together." Michael looked past me at the studio door. "I'd really like to see how the tape's coming. Can't I just take a peek?"

"Not while it's rendering," I said. "It's too delicate. It's extremely sensitive at this point. Just opening a screen, or even hitting a key, could cause a lockup or a crash. And I'd have to start all over. It could set me back a day.

"Well, let's not risk that."

He sniffed the air and made a face. "What's that stink?"

When I'd opened the door to leave the studio, some of the burning plastic odor had escaped.

"Oh, one of the Jazz drives overheated, I'm afraid. That happens on occasion. Thank God we've got several."

"Is it ruined?" He tried to step around me.

"Yes, it's ruined." I took his arm to stop him. "But let me show you in the morning. I don't want to go back in there tonight, not while the clip is rendering. I had to tiptoe out. Believe me, I've seen these things mess up just from a minor vibration. It's a very delicate process."

He stopped. "You're right," he said. "Better safe than sorry. You're sure everything is OK, though? There's no fire danger?"

"No, no. I lost a Jazz disk, but I had a copy. And the drive's unplugged now. Nothing to worry about. It smells a lot worse than it is."

Michael hesitated. He looked tired and a bit unfocused, as if he'd also put in a long day. "Well, it *is* late." He yawned. "I suppose everything can wait until morning. By the way, I want to thank you again for stepping in."

"I believe in America," I said earnestly.

"Indeed." We'd reached a fork in the path. "Well, good night, Bill. You'd best get some sleep. If you're hungry, if there's anything you need—"

"Thanks. I had a sandwich around 8. I think all I need now is a pillow for my head."

"You're not alone there." He smiled and hugged me in the usual awkward way, avoiding any chance of crotch contact. "God bless you, Bill. Sleep well."

Once Michael was out of sight, I moved quickly. Back to my room, where I pulled on khakis and a fresh cotton shirt, and quickly stuffed the remainder of my things into my satchel, which also contained—I hoped—a usable version of Revelations. The *only* usable version. I climbed into the Ford Explorer they were letting me use now, and approached the final obstacle: the guard booth at the compound gate.

A chubby bot in navy blue shorts and matching tennis shirt stepped out as I stopped. With a walkie-talkie hooked to his belt and a holstered revolver, he resembled an L.A. beach-patrol cop. By this time it was almost 1 in the morning, and he looked suspicious.

"Hi," I said. "Gotta run into town. To the all-night pharmacy. Ran out of blood pressure pills."

"Which pharmacy would that be, sir?"

"I don't remember the name. It's downtown."

"We can have it delivered, sir. If you're not feeling well."

"No, I'm fine right now," I said. "But I won't be by morning if I don't get a refill. Look, I've been working all day, cooped up in the video lab for 15 hours. Frankly, I kind of need to get into the wind, if you know what I mean."

I could see he sensed something not quite right, even though my tone was convincingly casual. Finally, though, he said, "Very well, sir. Have a pleasant drive." And he opened the gate.

I hopped the first flight out of Nashville, paying cash. By mid morning I was in Madison, Wis. With $37 and a walletful of easily traced and therefore unusable credit and ATM cards. In short, I was fucked. I couldn't even return to the Vault, since it was only a matter of time before Steve coughed up the address.

As I pondered my options, my cell phone rang. It was Steve.

"Jim?"

I heard traffic in the background. He was calling from a pay phone.

"What's up?"

"You're in trouble. *Big* trouble."

"Yeah?"

"Look, I'm back in Tennessee. I got back this morning. Michael is very mad at you. Because of what you did."

I must have just missed Steve at the Nashville airport.

"I don't know what you mean," I said.

"I'm only calling you because I know that in your own demonic way you tried to help me once. I'm calling to warn you. That Michael's very angry. And God will punish you."

"I can deal with God, thanks. But what's Michael up to?"

"Do you need a diagram? Use your imagination."

"I take it you've told him where I live."

"I had no choice."

"Right."

"You shouldn't have done what you did, Jim. You've made people very unhappy. Not just Michael. Others too. Who are much more powerful. You sabotaged a very elegant plan."

"I'd call it scummy, Steve, not elegant. Sleazy, vile, and scummy."

"I didn't have to make this call."

"Frankly, I don't see why you did. Did you think I wouldn't know these people were mad at me? You think this scares me? I've got news for you, fundie queer boy. If the day ever comes when I don't have somebody trying to kill me, I'll know it's time to retire."

"You may be retiring sooner than you'd like. They've dispatched some people to find you."

"I see." Finally some useful data. "Bots?"

"What?"

"*Robots.* Genesis robots."

"No," he said. "They hired it out. To a couple of Latinos. Beware of Latinos."

"Thanks. That narrows it down."

"One is cute. He has a goatee, like me. He's bisexual or whatever. He may try to pick you up. Understand?"

"Uh, yeah. That helps. I'll blow off goateed bisexual Latinos. Thanks."

"I'm serious, Jim. I shouldn't even be warning you. I don't like what you did. Destroying the program and the equipment and all that work. It was mean, Jim."

"I wish I thought you were kidding. I wish you *were* kidding. But I know you're not. What *Genesis* is doing is mean."

"Look, I have to get back. I can't talk any longer. I know it was sick and wrong and perverted, but I *did* feel something for you once. I only wish I'd introduced you to Jesus."

"Maybe next time."

"May God have mercy on your soul, Jim."

"Buh-bye, pumpkin. Watch out for Ed Keck."

Almost as soon as I hung up, the phone rang again. Linkletter.

"Listen," he said. "I know you were up there at Diane Rainey's the day she got her head chopped off. What I wanna know is *why*."

"I have no idea what you're talking about."

"We know you were there. Biff saw your Land Cruiser."

"The Palisades is full of Land Cruisers."

"Save it. We found your prints on the bathroom wall. I figure you braced yourself against it when you threw up. After you found her."

What could I say? "I didn't kill her."

"I believe you," he said. "But I can't say that Biff Decker shares my opinion."

"So I've heard."

"We've got no doubt the Russians did it. There are some facts we've been withholding."

"Figured. Other witnesses?"

"No comment. Now tell me what happened. And for once don't shit me."

"OK." I waited for an elderly couple to stroll past. "We spoke on the phone, and Diane invited me up to the house. When I got there, she was already cooking."

"And what exactly was your connection with her?"

I paused to consider the ramifications of telling him the truth. It seemed pointless to stonewall him.

So I told him about the diet pills. That I'd found them, given some to Diane, had some tested, and discovered the asbestos. How I'd overheard Biff's plans to have the pills manufactured in Mexico, despite the known health risks.

"So that's why you were in Europe," Linkletter said. "What exactly happened there?"

"You don't want to know."

He hesitated. "You just may be right about that. We *do* know what happened in Moscow, incidentally. Or at least the Russian version. Your friend Vlad didn't croak, by the way."

"So I've heard. I was hoping that information was wrong."

"Well, it isn't." We have strong reason to believe he's back in the U.S., with a major jones for you. Don't say you weren't warned."

"Thanks, Frank. It's good to have friends."

"So these pills, they really work?"

I pictured his huge gut and said, "If you don't mind getting cancer."

"But that takes years, right?"

"I don't know, Frank. I'm not a doctor. All I know is, I'm going to call the FDA."

"Well, I guess it's a question of ethics."

"So where's this going, Frank? I haven't told you anything you don't know yet."

"About to get to that. It's simple. I know it's been hard for you to keep your mouth shut about the Patti Grant deal. You put your ass on the line, and I know humility is not one of your virtues."

Linkletter had to know that I'd never really bought the cops' face-saving bullshit about the need to keep my involvement quiet while they tried to find and "rescue" Patti—especially when she so clearly had no desire to be rescued. He also had to know, as I did, that the story was too big, that it was bound to break.

And it had.

"Let me ask you something," Frank said. "Have you been to the market lately?"

"No. Why?"

"Watched TV?"

"I've been out of town."

"Yeah, I know. I can see I need to bring you up to speed. The story broke. Big-time. But here's the catch. She's in France, in the south of France, with Herschman, and they're still in lovebird mode. So she's denying the whole tit-bomb deal. They even got phony x-rays to prove it's a lie. She's saying it was a lie from the get-go, dreamed up by her speed-freak husband when she ran off with the doc."

"Which can only mean they haven't had their first fight. So what do you want from me?"

"To keep your mouth shut, no matter what happens. One of the print tabloids mentioned your role. We want you to deny it, for the sake of the department."

"And if I don't?"

"Don't be dense."

"I'm not. I just want to hear you say it."

"Well, your prints *are* linked to a murder..."

"You're a fuck."

"Plus I'll do what I can to get Biff off your case."

I decided he was actually not lying.

"All right," I said. "I can live with that. If you can keep Biff away from me. Until the feds can set up a sting. I don't give a shit if he's a star; if he's making those pills, he's going to prison."

"Right. Just like the Juice. Dream on."

"We'll see. Is that all?"

"For now. But watch your back. Vlad wants you bad."

As soon as I hung up, I called an official at the FDA, a man I will not name. I'll just say he's someone who's well-known to AIDS activists, which was how I'd met him, back in the days when I'd been involved with ACT UP. He was one of the FDA officials initially hostile to ACT UP's demands for new, speedier drug-testing protocols. But he came around, which ironically made him controversial to some in the gay community who saw him as one of the government officials who "neutralized" ACT UP by bringing some of its members on board as drug-policy consultants. Either way, I've always felt this guy's heart and mind were in the right place.

I told him about the diet pills in general terms—leaving out, for obvious reasons, the details of my European search. I presented it this way: "They were weight-loss pills made for Eva Braun by one of Hitler's doctors. Diane Rainey, who'd learned of their possible existence, hired me to find them, and I did."

"Oh, God," he said. "You're not involved in that whole Rainey mess, are you?"

"Only in the sense that I brought her some of the pills. Somehow the Russian Mafia got wind of it. They're the ones who killed her. You can ask the LAPD. The decapitation thing, that's their M.O. They wanted the pills because, here's the thing, they work. They are, in a sense, a weight-loss miracle drug. But there's an ugly catch. They contain asbestos."

"Asbestos? Are you sure?"

"Yes. Now here's why I'm telling you this. Biff Decker, who as you know is Diane's bereaved hubby, is trying to manufacture the pills anyway. I have an extremely incriminating recording of his side of a conversation with a Mexican drug maker, which I'm going to mail to you. Biff knows the pills are lethal, but he doesn't care. He wants to use them himself and give them to his Hollywood friends and God knows who else. Supposedly, he's going to tell people what's in the pills so they can make their own call, but I don't trust that he'll really do that. And, of course, if the Russians get the formula... Well, you can imagine the worldwide disaster. That's why I'm calling you. This has to be stopped."

I'll give the feds some credit. They didn't drag their feet with Biff. Six days later they busted him for conspiracy to manufacture and import illegal substances. Within a few days the TV media had copies of the sting tape: Biff and Jorge exchanging money and a cache of pills in a San Diego hotel room—and then the feds kicking in the door. "FBI! You're under arrest!"

As it turned out, Biff was busted paying for the second batch. The first one had been relatively small: 1,000 pills for Biff and Diane and their close friends to test. The batch he was caught with came in bottles of 100 tabs, with an Alpine design on the label and the single word: Berchedrine. The entire shipment, which filled a number of boxes, contained 600,000 pills.

Biff's massive PR spin could have been predicted. He hired the best attorneys, and his huge and loyal fan base readily bought his earnest claim of naïveté. OK, so he *had* "kind of" broken the law. He *had* been bringing in "technically" unauthorized weight-loss drugs, but not for sale, and who would think he'd need the money? Huh? And he'd had "no idea" what was in the pills, only that they seemed to work. It was *Jorge,* the evil, greasy, lying Mexican scumbag, who'd callously "tricked him," etc.

Biff was out of jail in less than two days, after a smitten female judge lowered his initial million-dollar bail to $100,000, for which he wrote a check. So he was back on the street and madder than ever. And, as I'd learn, he *still* thought I'd killed his nasty twitch-box wife.

Freakishly, after I hung up with Linkletter, Vlad called.

"Hey, fuck. You are a dead man, fuck. You fucked me up

real bad, but I am still going to finish what I fucking started. You get the drift, fuck?"

"I think so, Vlad," I said, affecting my usual foppish tone with him. "Despite the deliciously cryptic nature of your verbal missive. But you really must tell me how you survived that head wound, cupcake. Nothing short of a miracle, I'd say. Tell me, has it restored your faith in God?"

"Fuck God and fuck you and your faggoty shit, you fuck. You can plan your memorial and count off the hours until you fucking die."

"The first is already done, Vlad. I've had my memorial mapped out for years. Right down to my favorite song, 'Sister Ray' by the Velvet Underground. Eighteen bludgeoning minutes of pure sonic genius. Though I suspect some mourners won't last the duration. But you will, I trust. And I certainly hope that when your chance comes, you'll speak. About what it was like to cut off my head."

"Your head will be the last piece of shit to fucking go. As we cut off the other parts of your body, you will scream, beg, and whimper. Just like some other fucking pussies I don't got to mention."

"Vlad, I'm beginning to find this train of thought distasteful. I believe I shall terminate this call right now." I hung up.

And then I turned my cell phone off.

Still at the Madison airport, I sat down to think. To try to figure out how to stay alive on $37.

The waiting area had one of those televisions that plays only news. I looked at it and noticed a publicity photo of Patti Grant.

It seems Patti was in Cannes, promoting a film project. Or promoting herself, really. The usual Cannes swimsuit shtick for the horde of photographers. You know, smiling and posing in a thong on the beach, such as it is there. When suddenly her breasts exploded.

They caught it on tape, although the airport news wasn't showing it.

I saw a bootleg copy much later. It's really quite horrifying. She's smiling one moment, with those perfect, barely covered cantaloupe breasts. A second later they're exploding, blood splashing the camera lens. She's looking down, screaming. Her death, unfortunately, was not instantaneous.

"Jesus," I said, to no one in particular.

PART THREE
ANARCHY, OR, HOW I MET CATHERINE DENEUVE

Patti Grant's tits exploding was absolutely, completely, and totally as much as I could take. I strolled over to the airport bar and spent my remaining $37 getting drunk on Jack Daniel's. I don't remember stumbling back to the gate area and falling asleep. But apparently I did.

I woke up around midnight with a screaming headache.

I took stock of my situation. It was the middle of the night, my head ached, I had 51 cents in my pocket, and I was stranded in a city where I knew no one. Not to mention the fact that the Russian Mafia, a pair of Latinos, America's favorite action hero, and possibly neo-Nazis were all trying to kill me.

And then it hit me: A review of my novel *Tim and Pete.* An extremely positive review. From *American Anarchist,* a quarterly based in Madison.

I found a phone booth with a local directory and looked up

the listing for *American Anarchist,* but decided that would be a wasted phone call, since it was the middle of the night. I needed to reach the publisher at home, if I could remember his name. Harry something. Alder? No, Aldrich. That was it. I found a single listing. As I'd expected, the number was different, but the address was the same as the journal's. Not a big operation.

On the second ring, a gruff voice answered. "This better be fuckin' good."

"Is this Harry Aldrich?"

"Who wants to know?"

"Look, Harry, this is James Robert Baker. I don't know if you remember, but you reviewed one of my novels a while—"

"Who?"

"James Robert Baker. I wrote a book called *Tim and Pete."*

"Oh, yeah. Yeah, that. So why the fuck are you calling me at 1 o'clock in the morning?"

"Because I'm stranded here in Madison. At the airport. Long story. And I'm broke. Also a long story. I'm stranded."

Heavy sigh. "Fuck. So you want me to come and get you, is that it?"

"I know it's late. I know it's inconvenient. But I don't know anybody else in Madison."

"Christ. I was having a dream. A sex dream. You fucked it up."

"I'm sorry."

"OK, OK. Wait out by the curb. I don't wanna have to look for you. I'll be in a blue Volvo. Give me half an hour."

Ⓐ

I waited by the curb. It was a warm night, humid. I was dehydrated. I felt like refried shit. I felt the way the car looked when it finally pulled up: a scraped and battered late-'70s Volvo. But the driver was not the grizzled old leftist I'd expected. He was a younger man with shoulder-length blond hair, a darker goatee. He got out. He was tall, wearing baggy Levi's and a faded Rage Against the Machine T-shirt.

"Harry?"

He laughed softly. "I'm Todd. Harry's son. Welcome to Madison." He shook my hand and glanced at my satchel. "Is that all you've got? No other luggage?"

"That's it."

We climbed into the car.

As we pulled out, he said, "Jeez, you smell like a booze factory. You're not an alcoholic, are you?"

"Not generally, no."

"That's good," he said. "I'm a big fan of yours. I wrote the review you mentioned to my dad."

It came back to me, fuzzily, that the review had been written by a *Todd* somebody. But not Aldrich. "You have a different last name, right?"

"Yeah. Mulligan. My mom and dad never got married. You know how it was in the '60s."

I found it hard to look at Todd because he was so fucking attractive. Not movie-star handsome. Not vapid *Sea Crew* handsome. But he had blue eyes, a pink mouth I wanted to kiss, and a clarity to his pale skin that blew me out of the water. But I couldn't get a gaydar reading. Most of the time I can. But sometimes I can't. There's a certain kind of straight guy who seems so gentle-natured you could confuse it with something else. And to the extent that I was able to think much at all, I was putting Todd into that slot.

Of course, he *had* read *Tim and Pete.* But the novel had a lot of straight readers, especially open-minded, iconoclastic straights.

"Dad was going to come and get you," he said. "But he has some physical problems. A bad back and all that. And I was still awake, working. He wants to meet you in the morning, though. Looks like you're going to have to conk in my bed, if you don't mind. We're kind of running out of space lately."

"That's cool. Whatever."

"Things have been picking up quite a bit lately." His tone was buoyant, especially given the hour. "We've been revamping the journal. We're about to put out our new issue. I can show you in the morning. If you're interested."

In a while we pulled up to a weathered two-story house on a seedy residential street, where Todd parked in the driveway. As he led me back to the garage, we passed some windows where we could see other young people still up and working on the journal, even though by now it was past 2 in the morning.

"You see what I mean?" Todd said. "A lot of activity. Dad was kind of spooked at first. Set in his ways and all that. But now he's very pleased. It's kind of touching, really. He told me the other night he was afraid he'd die before he saw this happen. And it almost didn't."

"What do you mean?"

We reached the side door of the garage, which he'd converted into an apartment. There were rock and political posters on the walls, a mattress with a faded blue-and-white quilt on the floor. It looked like a crash pad from the '60s. Except instead of Jimi Hendrix's image on the wall, there was Trent Reznor's.

Todd went to a small refrigerator, where he took out a pitcher of tea and poured me a large glass. "Well, take me for example," he said. "And drink this. You look dehydrated. It's OK. It's chamomile. It won't keep you awake."

I gulped down the tea. "Thanks."

"I mean, I'm 37, OK?" he said. "And I started the '80s as a total Reagan fascist. I went to Harvard and studied business. Of course, I'd been brought up by my mother after she left dad in the '70s. She'd totally recanted her radical ways and all that. I mean, she's Catholic, so she married this asshole contractor in Boston, who turned her into a human incubator. So now I have 10 brothers and sisters. Not all from Mom. My stepfather was married before. But I think that's a big reason why she accepts my being gay—to the extent that she does. It's not like I'm gonna doom the family line."

I was startled by the casual way he'd dropped this information. And I sensed that he might be attracted to me. But I was hoping he wasn't going to come on to me right away, since I was not at my best.

"God, I feel bad," I said. "You mind if I have some more tea?"

He poured me another glass. "Anyway, that's what changed me eventually. I got my degree and moved to Manhattan and became—what else?—a stockbroker. Then my boyfriend got sick. Jay. He got sick just as ACT UP was starting. And I got involved with that. Very deeply involved. It changed my outlook on everything. Jay died in '94. I'm still negative, by the way. I only moved back here about six months ago because Dad was about to shut down the journal. Jesus, you look exhausted. You wanna go to bed? I didn't mean to talk your ear off."

"That's OK. But I think I would like to go to bed. Do you have some Excedrin or something?"

"Got some Advil, I think. Let me check."

He looked through the vitamin pill bottles on the counter of the makeshift kitchen area. "You're in luck."

I took four pills and had another glass of tea. Then he lowered the lights and we got undressed for bed. I left my boxers on. He wasn't wearing any, so he climbed into bed beside me naked. Then he shut off the light.

We both lay there silently for a while. You could say there was some tension. Not a bad tension, though. Finally, he said, "Look, I know you're out of it tonight. But I hope we can get better acquainted in the morning. And who knows, maybe I can even get you to stick around for a while. We could definitely use you. As a writer, I mean. And beyond that..." He touched my arm. "You know, whatever."

The next thing I knew we were hugging. And he had a hard-on. I didn't. I was too wiped out. He kissed me lightly on the lips and said, "Good night. Do you go by James or Jim?

"Jim's OK. Good night, Todd."

He kissed me again, then rolled away. "Sleep well."

I did.

I met Harry the next morning at breakfast, along with everybody else in the group. Harry was pretty much as I'd expected: a paunchy, white-haired Jewish guy who reminded me a lot of Norman Mailer, if Mailer had a white goatee. "My back's bad, my heart's bad, my liver's shot, I've got stomach problems," he said as he wolfed down his huge breakfast. "If it weren't for these kids, I'd probably be dead now. Six months ago I was ready to throw in the towel."

"Harry, chill on the butter if you wanna be around to see the new issue come out," Brigitte said. She was a young lesbian with slicked-back black hair and several wire-like rings in each ear. And a girlfriend, Ellen, who had a blond buzz cut. There was one other gay guy, Paco, a graphic artist. But the others in the group, John, Sara, Marshall, Jed, Michelle, and Gary were straight. Michelle and Gary were a couple. They were all a little punchy from putting in long hours to meet the new edition's deadline. It was going to the printer in less than two days.

After breakfast, Todd showed me the new layout on his computer. He also had some sample printouts, which he compared to the stodgy old newsprint version. A dramatic change for the better. Todd referred vaguely to an "infusion of capital." I didn't ask for specifics, but clearly the infusion was significant. What they were going to put out was not a cheap product. Todd also talked about a new line of distribution.

"We'll be on newsstands next to *The New Republic* and right-wing crap like *The American Spectator.* We *will* be noticed. I can promise you that."

I agreed, and not just because they had good graphics. The articles I read were incisive and pulled no punches. The new issue featured two major pieces: one on Blockbuster Video and its censorious practices and pernicious influence on American films; another on the scummy business dealings of televangelist and presidential wannabe Pat Robertson. A lot of what I read was, in a general sense, not new to me. But they were stories avoided by the mainstream media, despite its alleged liberal bias. Of course, I'd always felt that right-wing charge was kind of a joke, given how the media handled, for example, vile theocratic slime like Ed Keck with kid gloves.

"Yeah, I think you're going to get some attention," I said. "I hope you're aware of how dangerous some of these people can be."

"Oh, we expect to be sued," Todd said. "We're ready for that."

"That's not what I meant."

He gave me a funny look. "What do you mean? That they might try to kill us?"

I had to consider how much I wanted to reveal about my situation. I decided it was too soon to tell him too much. "Don't misunderstand me," I said. "I'm not trying to discourage you. On the contrary, I support what you're doing. I think this stuff needs to come out. But you should be aware that even some of the allegedly sane right-wingers have close ties to militia groups and others who think nothing of violence."

Todd looked around. We were in his office in the main house, and there were other people in adjoining rooms, but they were out of earshot. "Look," he said, "we're anarchists, not pacifists. We're fully aware of what the other side can do. And we're prepared. There's a lot I haven't told you yet, because I'm not sure how much you want to know."

I smiled. "There's a lot I haven't told *you*."

He laughed lightly. "I had that feeling. Maybe we should start trusting each other a little bit." He put his arms around me. And kissed me. I was aware that others of the group could see us, but they were busy, and nobody gave us a second look.

We kept kissing until we both got pretty turned-on. "You wanna go out to the garage?" he said.

"Sounds good to me."

Afterward, Todd said, "I hope you don't have to get back to L.A. anytime soon."

"To tell you the truth..." I ran my hand over the hair on his chest, which, like his beard, was dark instead of blond. "I'm ready to kiss off L.A. It's been my home for a long time, most of my life. But I've got serious problems there."

"Like what?"

"Like people mad at me. I don't feel safe there anymore."

He seemed to consider asking me to elaborate, before deciding against it. Instead he said, "Why don't you stay here?"

"OK."

"Good." He kissed me. "That's solved."

"Only one thing. I need to go back to L.A. to get some stuff."

"Like what?"

"Just some things. Personal items," I said, as I picked up a notepad and wrote, "Let's go for a walk. This place could be bugged."

He nodded, not smiling or laughing as if I were being paranoid, which was what I'd expected. Then he said, "That sounds fine. Oh, by the way, I need to hit the market. Wanna come along?"

"Sure."

As we walked down a shady residential street, he said, "I don't really think we're being bugged. Not yet anyway. But there's no point in taking chances, especially if we're dealing with something that might be...illicit. What's on your mind?"

I waited until we'd turned the corner and I'd scanned the street for any sort of van that could have been an undercover surveillance vehicle. But there were just parked cars. So I said, "Have you ever heard of a right-wing Christian group in Tennessee called Genesis?"

He stopped walking. "Yeah. They're computer geeks. Why?"

"Well...I infiltrated them."

"Are you kidding? When?"

So, while we walked down the street and then through a small park, I told him the whole story. And by the *whole story,* I mean just that, beginning with the O.J. tape. The only part I left out was the blow job from Ed Keck. I mentioned *meeting* Ed, but I couldn't bring myself to let Todd know that Keck had ever wrapped his evil right-wing lips around my member.

"So that's why you're afraid to go back to L.A.," Todd said.

"Because Russians, neo-Nazis, naked fundies, and Biff Decker are out for your blood."

"Correct."

"So why is it that you want to go back?"

"To get the money that Diane paid me."

"Let it sit," he said. "I told you, the journal is flush."

"I know. But I don't like freeloading. And it's more than 200 grand. That kind of money can be useful. Even when you're flush."

"True."

"So," I said. "How do you feel about all this?"

"What do you mean?"

"Well, as far as I know, nobody knows where I am. Which doesn't mean people aren't looking for me. That they won't find me and try to kill me. And possibly you and your dad and Brigitte and everybody else."

He smiled. "Remember when I said there's a lot I haven't told you? Well..." He looked around. "Let me put it like this. When your enemy is using chemical weapons, you can't expect to beat them with a slingshot. When we get back to the house, I'll show you where the guns are. We're not Gandhi freaks."

"Good. You show me the weapons, and I'll show you the Revelations program."

"Ah," he said. "You show me yours and I'll show you mine."

"I think we did that this morning."

"We could do it tonight too," he said. "I don't want to get mushy or anything, so I won't. But it's cool you're sticking around."

I was beginning to feel the same way.

That night while I was sitting on Todd's mattress watching the news on his small TV, he came in with a nine-millimeter machine pistol. "We can keep this by the bed. Will that help you sleep?"

"Won't hurt."

Then he told me he was going to discuss the Revelations program with only one other person: Brigitte, because she knew the most about computers. "I'm not going to tell anyone else. Including Dad. He's kind of a technophobe, for starters. Beyond that, I think it's the sort of thing he'd rather not know about. He has an old-fashioned belief that you should always fight fair. I don't agree."

"I think you're right," I said. "Wimps end up in mass graves."

The next morning Todd and I had sex again, and it was even better than the first time. And I knew it was going to keep getting better.

Afterward, I said, "You know, I should go back to L.A. soon. Maybe Brigitte can salvage Revelations while I'm gone."

"I'll go with you."

"No. Forget it."

"I knew you'd say that," he said. "I can still help, though. You're going to need a new ID, new credit cards and all that. I can get those for you."

"You know how to do that?"

"Yeah. Don't worry. It'll take a few days, but it's no problem."

"Great," I said. "That should make things pretty easy."

"I still think I should come with you."

"Not happening. Look, I'm not going near the place where I was staying. Even though I hate to lose all my clothes and my notes and a novel in progress and my CDs and stuff."

"Just remember," he said, "I want you back here alive. In case I decide to fall in love with you or something weird like that."

"I don't want to spook you, but from my side, that's already kind of happening."

"I know." He kissed me. "From my side too."

I came into L.A. through the Burbank airport wearing a cheap business suit. I was also clean-shaven, even though the Genesis people knew me that way. But everybody else knew me—and all of my recent photos showed me—with a goatee or full beard. The dorky glasses and bad conservative crew cut also made me look surprisingly different. We'd experimented with fake buckteeth, but they kept slipping out when I talked, so we canned them.

My new ID, including an Ohio driver's license and several credit cards, was John Reed, from Toledo. Since both my mother and father were born in Ohio, and I still have relatives there, including a miserable alcoholic closet-case cousin, I looked much the way I might've looked, and been, had my parents not come to California in the '50s. Stuck in Ohio, I could well have ended up like my lonely "bachelor" cousin.

I was scheduled for a flight back in a little more than three hours, so I had no time to spare. I rented a car, a Dodge Neon, and headed directly to my bank in Woodland Hills, where I planned to close out the account that held all but $10,000 of what was left of the money Diane Rainey had paid me: a little over 200 grand. I was going to ask for a cashier's check made out to a friend of Todd's in Georgia—a woman he knew well and trusted. For this reason I'd also brought my real California driver's license.

I entered the bank, filled out the withdrawal slip, and got in line.

Given the large sum, I was braced for a talk with a bank vice president or manager or whoever. I was not, however, prepared for what happened. The teller punched in my account number and said, "Mr. Baker, I'm sorry. According to our records, you closed this account last week."

"That's impossible. Are you sure you've got the right account?"

He read off my Topanga address. And I said, "Yes, that's me."

"According to our records, you closed out the account last Wednesday at our Rolling Hills branch."

"That's impossible," I said again.

"That's what our records show."

"I'd like to speak to whoever's in charge here."

That turned out to be a beautiful but icy female vice president. I said, "Look, I've been robbed. Somebody's raided my account."

She looked up the account on her desktop computer. "I don't see how that could happen, Mr. Baker. Anyone who wanted to withdraw a sum that large would have to show a photo ID. Would you mind if I saw yours?"

I handed her my driver's license, where I had a goatee. She looked at it, at me, skeptically.

"It's me, OK?" I took off my dorky glasses. "I am James Robert Baker, and someone has robbed me of $200,000."

She looked at my driver's license, then at the data on her screen. "Well, Mr. Baker, if you didn't close your account, someone with a driver's license with your number on it did. Do you have anything else with your photo? A company ID or—"

"No. I'm a writer. We don't wear a clip-on ID."

She handed my license back. "I'm afraid I really don't know what to tell you."

"Look, you don't get it. How many times do I have to tell you? I did not make any withdrawal from Rolling Hills." And then it hit me as I said it: "Someone's hacked my account!"

Vlad.

"I'm sorry, Mr. Baker. If you want to pursue this matter, I can give you our 800 number."

"I don't want your fucking 800 number! I want my fucking money!"

I realized I was shouting and that everybody in the bank was looking at me. I also realized that drawing attention to myself was a bad idea. But I was still steamed.

I got up. "This is outrageous. Someone's hacked my account, and if you think you can cover up this breach in security, you're in for a big surprise. I suggest you call your fucking 800 number and get this matter straightened out. Or you're going to be facing a PR debacle, not to mention a very serious lawsuit."

That seemed to shake her a bit—the PR debacle, probably. "Mr. Baker, if what you're saying is true, I understand your distress. I *will* have the matter looked into immediately. Are you still at your Topanga address?"

"No," I said. "I'm unreachable."

And then I left. As quickly and as quietly as I could.

In the sun-baked Neon, I rolled down the windows, turned the air conditioner up full-blast, and took off. I tried to calm myself but couldn't. It occurred to me that it could have been Genesis, since they knew who I was now, and Steve, when he was living with me, could've easily snagged my bank account and license numbers. And Genesis clearly had the wherewithal to make up phony IDs. To a reasonable mind, they were the most logical suspects. And yet I smelled Vlad.

Wigged-out or not, I had no time to waste. I headed south on Topanga Canyon Boulevard, took a left at Mulholland, and within a few minutes I was up in the hills on Old Topanga Road, a narrow, winding, two-lane blacktop with very little traffic.

In the quiet of the canyon I chilled out as much as I could, knowing I could at least retrieve the $10,000 and the useless copy of the O.J. tape I'd buried.

I pulled over in a desolate stretch of chaparral-covered hills and parked. I took a hard-plastic fold-up shovel—basically an entrenching tool—from my carry-on bag and opened it. Then I walked several hundred feet through a grove of eucalyptus trees to a small clearing—an area where people came to fuck and party. The ground was littered with beer cans and torn condom foils. Using a chalky rock to get my bearings, I found the spot, back behind a brace of chaparral, and started digging.

I hadn't buried the bag that deeply and the earth was still loose. Within a minute I had the bag and was headed back to my rental car.

That's when I saw Vlad and four other Russians.

All of them were wearing cheap polyester casual attire, as if they'd just gone on a shopping binge at Kmart. Their machine pistols looked cheap too, like toys. But of course they weren't, and they all had one, including Vlad, who held his awkwardly. He took a dragging step toward me and said, "Hey, fuck. What you got in the bag?"

"Vlad, darling. How nice to see you."

"Some magic pills maybe? Or something else good? Huh? Let's see. You toss the bag over here."

My heart pounded like a rivet gun. I really saw no way out this time. "I don't have any of those pills, Vlad. You know I turned them over to the FDA. They're useless now. As useless as the O.J. tape. You gutted Diane Rainey for nothing."

"You are wrong as always, fuck," he said. "I don't care if she got the pills. I gut her for the hell of it. Before I cut off her fucking head. I only want to see what a movie star have for lunch." Harsh laugh. "Some kind of fucking pasta. Fucking angel-hair crap. Enough to feed a fucking pig." He laughed again.

"Vlad, dearie. You are one twisted piece of shit."

"And you are dead, fuck. Unless you throw the bag over."

I had zero doubt they were going to kill me anyway. But I tossed the bag toward them to buy time, on the off chance I could think of a way out.

They were still some distance from me—maybe 50 feet away. Vlad signaled one of his comrades to retrieve the bag and open it. As his pal took out the Juice cassette, Vlad said, "You fuck. You dirty fuck. I knew you still have this."

"I don't recall ever saying I didn't," I said. "But as I've pointed out to you many times, precious, the tape, while technically flawless, is wrong. There's a major error in the action. It won't play, cupcake."

"*What* fucking error?"

"Now why should I tell you that with those popguns aimed at me? You chaps put those silly things down and we'll go grab some lunch. I'm famished. And *then* I'll tell you."

"There's nothing wrong with this tape," Vlad said.

"Vlad, darling, what's the point in arguing now? When you're about to kill me? I know the tape is a fraud. It was made by those sexy people at Genesis."

Vlad flared. "Those fucking Christians! You think I—"

Our discussion was cut short by Vlad's buddy pulling my $10,000 from the bag.

And any chance of discussing that was cut short by a fusillade of automatic weapons fire.

I dove for the nearest cover, a dry creek bed, without looking back. But I could hear Vlad and his buddies yelling in pain and hitting the ground. I don't think any of them even got off a shot.

From the creek bed I peeked back through the bushes and saw three male Caucasians with AK-47s. They were all in their late 40s with the look of ex-marines. They were dressed incongruously (I suppose) in golfing attire. Vlad was on the ground, badly wounded but still moving. One of the men stepped over to him, aimed his weapon point-blank at Vlad's head and said, "This is for Diane Rainey."

Pop!

I ducked after that. I badly wanted to take off running, but I knew if I did I'd make enough noise to draw their attention. I heard another *pop.* Apparently someone else had also still been alive.

Then one of them said, "He's gotta be around here somewhere."

So they knew I was there. Or that *somebody* was there. Whether they knew it was me by name, I couldn't determine. But my guess was they didn't. It seemed clear they'd been hired by Biff, who apparently had finally been persuaded that Vlad had killed his wife. So they'd been on Vlad's tail.

How Vlad managed to be so close on *my* tail I'll never know for sure.

I heard one of them walk toward where I was hiding. I heard the guy standing right above me, scanning the creek bed, his weapon no doubt ready.

One of the other guys called to him, "Anything?"

"No."

Then there were sirens in the distance, faint but growing. Even though there weren't any homes in the immediate area, sound carried in the hills, and someone must have reported the gunfire.

"Fuck it," one of the men said. "Let's go."

Cautiously, I peered through the bushes again in time to see one of the men pick up my $10,000, which at that point was lying on the ground near Vlad. He ignored the videocassette. Then he took off to catch up with his two buddies.

A few seconds later I heard them tear out.

I scooped up the cassette, trying not to look at Vlad and his dead pals.

I took off toward the freeway, even though that meant passing the cops as they approached. But I figured the killers probably headed south toward the beach, in the opposite direction of the cops, and at this point the police were less of a threat than hired killers. And besides, I had no time to spare if I planned to catch my flight.

Within a few minutes, four black-and-whites roared past me, lights flashing, sirens warbling. In my stodgy car, with my white shirt and tie, they paid me no mind.

Somehow I kept it together until I reached the freeway. Then I had a delayed reaction—even though, or perhaps because, I finally felt somewhat safe—and I nearly had a panic attack. Luckily, Todd had given me some Xanax. I dug the bottle out of my bag and chewed up three tablets dry.

By the time I reached Burbank and boarded my plane, nothing could bother me—not even the image of Vlad with the top of his head blown off. This time he was done. There'd be no getting up and stuffing his brains back in his skull.

When I came into the garage apartment, Todd was watching TV and looked pale.

"Thank God." He hugged me. "I've been going crazy. Couldn't you call?"

"Couldn't risk it."

We hugged for a long time. The TV was showing a commercial at first. Then it returned to a tabloid show.

"I thought you might be dead," Todd said, "and they just hadn't found you yet. After what happened to Biff Decker."

"What? What happened to Biff Decker."

"You haven't heard?"

"Heard what?"

But Todd didn't have to answer. The TV did it for him. On the screen was a shot of LAPD cops and firemen standing by a sheet-covered body alongside a canyon road. It didn't look like Topanga, though, and it wasn't. "The film star was found this afternoon by hikers in Tuna Canyon, not far from Pacific Coast Highway. According to police, Decker was shot in the back of the head, execution style..."

"Jesus," I said. "Do they know who did it?"

Todd shushed me and pointed to the TV. "Another hiker, who has requested anonymity, heard the shot and saw three male Caucasians speeding away from the scene in a dark gray sport-utility vehicle. Possibly a Toyota 4Runner or Nissan Pathfinder..."

"Oh, Christ," I said. "It's the guys who killed Vlad."

"*What?*"

I told Todd what had happened in L.A., starting with the bank.

"Holy shit."

"Exactly."

"I shouldn't have let you go there alone."

"Todd, that's probably what saved me. The clump of shrub I was hiding behind was barely big enough to hide *me.* If you'd gone, we'd both be dead."

"Maybe," he said.

"The way I see it, Biff finally realized it was Vlad who offed his wife. So he hired these three guys to whack Vlad. Who knows where he met them? He was *very* right-wing, so they could be militia types. Or maybe he just met them at the fucking gun range. I think I just happened to be there when they caught up with Vlad and iced him."

"You don't think Biff was looking for you too?"

"He probably was. Even if I didn't off his wife, I did finger him on the pill thing. But I don't think it matters now. He probably tried to stiff the killers the way Diane stiffed me. And they popped him. Anyway, I don't think the militia guys know I was the one there when they smoked Vlad and his pals. They know somebody was, but they didn't exactly give Vlad a chance to ID me. So I think we can scratch soldiers of fortune off the list of people trying to kill me."

"Maybe. What about the Russians?"

I shrugged. "I think Vlad was the one with the most serious hard-on for me. And I think his fellow Mafioski are going to realize I wasn't among the squad of gun freaks that wasted him and his pals. I don't think I'm going to be a major obsession for them. But I won't be taking any more trips to Moscow, just to be on the safe side."

"That leaves Genesis."

"Yeah," I said. "Genesis."

"I suppose you're never going to see that money again."

"Not unless I go back to L.A. As myself. And make a big enough stink."

"Probably not a good idea."

"Probably not."

We lay quietly on the bed, holding each other for several

minutes. Then he said, "By the way, Brigitte was able to load and open Revelations. We think it's usable. But we decided to wait for you to come back before trying it. Just in case. We don't want to fuck it up."

"That's cool," I said. "I'll give the two of you a run-through tomorrow. I'm too tired now."

After that we made love, and then I fell into a deep sleep.

After breakfast I gave Todd and Brigitte a quick overview of the Revelations program. Then I popped the O.J. tape into the VCR. They were appropriately impressed.

"This is amazing," said Todd. "*Ray,* was it?"

"Yeah, good old Ray."

"Well, he may have been fucked up, but he was a genius."

"I know. Too bad the fundies got him."

Brigitte said, "Are you sure this isn't real?"

"Yeah." I pointed out the throat-slashing error.

When the tape was done, we returned to the computer, where I brought up the Stinson-Perkins clip and showed them how the program worked.

Just for the fun of it, Todd opened a picture file of George W. Bush and put his head on Perkins' body. Then he picked some facial expression options and launched what the program called a Motivate. Within a few minutes the program rendered a sequence that ran as a realistic 20-second full-motion image of George W. silently wincing and groaning while he got fist-fucked.

Todd laughed. "This is incredible."

"Powerful," said Brigitte. "As a creative device *or* as a weapon."

"That's how Genesis was using it," I said. "As a weapon."

"You don't think they have backup copies?" said Todd.

"I doubt it. I'm sure they *had* backups. But I blowtorched all their software and discs and drives. And I got the feeling from Steve that I'd completely wiped them out."

I watched a sly smile spread across Todd's face. I knew him well enough by now to know what he was thinking. "We could have some serious fun with this. Some very serious fun."

"I think so too. But you're sure? No qualms?"

"Fuck, no."

"Brigitte?"

"If this had existed back in the '30s," she said, "you could've faked a clip of Hitler eating Eva Braun's shit and saved millions of lives. No, I don't have any qualms."

I mentioned Ed Keck's mentor, the foul right-wing televangelist Bud Chaswell. "Why not show him eating his wife's shit?"

"It would make more sense if he went to a hooker," said Todd. "Like Jimmy Swaggart."

"True," I said.

"That could be our first clip," said Brigitte. "If you guys have the stomach for it."

"Actually, it *is* pretty disgusting," I said. "I can think of things I'd rather do than spend hours tweaking a digital turd."

"You know what? It's probably too much," said Todd. "The shit thing, I mean. A lot of people might have a problem even *looking* at something like that."

"I would," I said.

"Pantywaist," said Brigitte.

"I am *not* a pantywaist."

"Exactly my point," said Todd. "We *want* people to look at this. Conservative middle-American people. That's why I think piss might be better. It's still enough to turn their stomachs in Des Moines, but it's not an instant puke inducer."

"I'd be more comfortable with that," I said. "Although it might be trickier technically."

"I'm game," said Brigitte.

"We could do it," Todd said. "I mean, the O.J. tape was pretty awesome. And a lot more complicated than just a golden shower."

"OK," I told them. "For starters, we'll need all the footage of Chaswell we can get. Then we're going to need a shot of a woman squatting down to take a pee."

"Brigitte?" said Todd.

"No problem." She smiled. "I know some riot grrrls in San Francisco. They collect stuff like that. Suicides, scat, bestiality... You name it, they've got it."

"All right," I said. "Bud Chaswell taking a golden shower. It's less extreme, but still twisted enough to scuttle his political career."

"That's what we need," said Todd. "An adultery thing wouldn't be enough. He has to look like a freak hiding behind his religion."

"For all we know," I said, "that's what he is."

"He wouldn't be the first," said Brigitte.

"By the way," said Todd, "this *really* has to stay among just us. I know this would freak out my father. I mean, I love him because he is who he is. He's decent and moral and above-board. But that's also why he almost went down for the count."

"No problem," I said.

"Ditto," agreed Brigitte.

Todd turned to Brigitte. "Can you get the piss tape without telling your friends what it's for?"

"Sure. They owe me a couple of favors."

I thought about Chaswell, his virulent homophobia. "You're sure it should be a woman?"

"In his case, yeah," Todd said. "If we were dealing with his darling little protégé, Ed Keck, I'd go for a guy. I get a strong closet-case vibe from him."

"Yeah," I said, "I think that might be part of his pre-born-again past."

"Hmm," said Todd. "Something to think about. Keck's a dangerous character. And he's cleaning himself up now. Trying to publicly distance himself from the serious fundie loonies. No doubt he wants to run for office."

"That's a safe bet," I said. "And deep down he's a total Nazi."

The next several weeks were a welcome lull in my life. Todd and I grabbed as much Bud Chaswell footage as we could, mostly from Bud's own show on the Jesus Channel. And John, it turned out, had an extensive archive of Chaswell footage, stuff he'd been taping for years, including many different angles of Chaswell on the campaign trail stumping for George W. Bush. It was in these tapes that we finally hit the jackpot: a low-angle shot looking up at our man from directly below a podium. High-quality tape and just the right angle. We could easily lift his head and place it under a squatting woman.

Brigitte busied herself with locating a good piss tape, which her friends in San Francisco actually didn't have. But they *were* able to get it. And when we watched the tape for the first time, we saw that it was perfect. An easy match with the footage we had of Chaswell. And the tape was just that—tape, as opposed to some aged grainy Super 8 film, as I'd feared. And while its quality was not as fine as the Betacam stuff of Chaswell, we could run both tapes through a series of filters to make everything look the same.

I ended up doing a lot of the work with Brigitte, since Todd was needed by the journal. She caught on fast, and as a result of the time we spent together, I got to know her much better.

She'd met Todd in ACT UP in New York. "It was heady at first," she said. "But as ACT UP became *absorbed,* for lack of a better word, some of us realized there was much more to be dealt with than just AIDS. I mean, the way it is now, the country is basically teetering on the edge of a fascist takeover." She said all this in a low-key way as she tweaked Chaswell's face, frame by frame.

"I know what you mean."

"Jim, look at this and tell me," she said. "Do you think the urine's too yellow?"

She ran a sequence of tape that showed canary yellow rain falling from nowhere, since the woman wasn't in the picture yet.

"Yeah, I think it's too bright. I mean, it shouldn't be Day-Glo."

She laughed and adjusted the hue to make it even brighter. "You don't think so? You don't think he'd like fluorescent pee?"

Ⓐ

The next morning I did what I'd been doing since my arrival in Madison. I went jogging through the nearby park. Before all of this started, I'd exercised regularly. Since then, except for a brief period of using Phil's home gym at the Vault, I hadn't done anything. But now that I was settled in, I'd begun a new regimen.

I'd felt safe in Madison since my arrival, as opposed to the escalating paranoia I'd felt in L.A. So I noticed the difference—an uneasy feeling—as I cut through sunny James Madison Park on the shore of glistening Lake Mendota. And then I saw why.

Sitting on a bench in a Madras shirt and khakis, waiting for me, was Ed Keck.

When I came to him, I stopped and said, winded, "What are *you* doing here?"

He smiled knowingly. "What do you think, Jim? I came to see you. Nobody but you."

I looked for any sign of others with him. He appeared to be alone. "What's on your mind, Ed?"

"Quite a lot, actually. You can relax, by the way. I came here alone."

"OK. Why?"

"I want your help," he said. "I want to make a deal with you."

A young couple strolled past us.

Ed gestured toward the walkway that ran the length of the park. "Perhaps we should walk. This is not the most private spot."

He got up and started walking. I was still on red alert. But there were a lot of people around, and if he wanted me dead, he wouldn't have shown up himself.

So I walked with him.

"How did you find me?"

"Let's just say it wasn't easy, and that nobody else knows where you are...yet. Though as you can imagine, Genesis would dearly love to find you. If you come through for me, though, I'll call them off. I can do that. You might want to keep that in mind as you hear what I have to say."

He waited with irritation as some kids ran past, chasing their golden retriever.

Then he said, "All right, here it is. Years ago, in the '80s, I spent some time in Los Angeles. This was before I found Christ, before he turned my life around. I had a job with a major corporation initially, a good job. But I was using speed. At first on weekends, then more frequently. Eventually, I lost my job. I went on unemployment, and then that ran out. By then I was so heavily addicted I'd do anything for a fix. And I did some things I'm not proud of, to put it mildly." Here, he paused, then said, "Including a porno tape."

"A *gay* porno tape?"

He nodded. "I was desperate. I did it for $300. Fortunately, the video was never released. Had it been, someone would no doubt have spotted me in it long ago, and I would've been cooked. But the producer died of AIDS before he could finish the project, and it was shelved. I believe he was a friend of yours, a fellow student at UCLA film school. Donny Boehm."

"Jesus." Rachel's late brother. "Yeah," I said. "I knew Donny. Not well, but I knew him."

"Well, I don't know if you knew he made these tapes. He used a pseudonym, of course. As I've come to understand it, he led a double life of sorts. On the one hand, he did his video art, which garnered him some critical praise and attention. And he also made rock videos. He financed his artier work by grinding out porn. Tapes that exploited desperate, strung-out young men."

"Like you."

"Like me. I believe you're friends with his sister, Rachel."

It seemed pointless to deny it. "Yes. So?"

"So when Donny died, he didn't leave a will. By California law, his estate went to his next of kin. In this case, his father. An Orange County Republican who'd disowned him some years before for being homosexual."

"I knew about that," I said. "About his father, I mean."

Ed squinted into the sunlight reflecting off the lake. "I'll be frank. I've had my people speak with your friend Rachel. They offered her a great deal of money for the tape. But she said her father destroyed all of Donny's work as soon as it fell into his hands. According to Rachel, her father destroyed everything. Not just the pornography but his art videos as well."

"It's possible," I said. I'd heard similar horror stories: relatives destroying novels and so forth. Works of art that weren't even pornographic, just gay-themed.

"The people who spoke with Rachel, however, came back with the distinct impression that she'd been less than forthcoming. They were nicely dressed gentlemen in suits and ties, and they spoke with her quite calmly and gently. Per my instructions. But when the talk turned to porno tapes, she exhibited signs of fear. My theory is this: It's quite possible that Donny was making these tapes for the criminal element. I hesitate to use the term Mafia, but the fact remains, the tape in question may not have been destroyed. And I strongly suspect Rachel knows more than she told my people. As her friend, perhaps you can get it out of her."

We walked down to the shore of the crystalline lake, where a breeze hit my sweaty torso, giving me a chill.

I said, "And if I do?"

"If you can locate the tape for me, you'll no longer have to worry about Genesis. And there will be a reward."

"Reward? How much?"

"A million dollars, any way you want it. Cash. Or in an offshore account."

I remained poker-faced, but inside I was slack-jawed.

"As you know," he said, "I have ambitions, plans. I *will* run for office. For senator or governor initially, and then president. To that end, I have—at great expense—cleaned up everything that could possibly come back to haunt me. Except for this tape. This is the last piece of unfinished business. The only thing standing between myself and the presidency."

I could argue that he was oozing megalomania and delusions of grandeur, but was he?

"I've already amassed far more power than you can imagine," he said. "I've learned a great deal from studying the strategy of a man with whom I have a few things in common: J. Edgar Hoover."

"You have files on everyone?"

"On my enemies and my allies. I just want to make sure none of *them* has a file on *me*."

"Well," I said, "I'll have to think about it."

"Take as much time as you need. But keep in mind, there will be repercussions if you decline. Very unpleasant repercussions."

"Is that a threat?"

He arched an eyebrow.

"You should chill on arching your eyebrows. It makes you look queeny. Like Truman Capote."

"I'll keep that in mind."

"I don't really have any choice, do I?"

"Actually, no."

"Fine," I said. "Let me talk to Rachel."

"Excellent," he said. "The tape may be labeled *After Gym Class.* That was the working title. As well as the setting. One of the guys was a bit older. In his 30s. He played the coach. I was one of the students."

"Were you a bad boy, Ed? Did you get spanked?"

"Just find the tape."

Todd was eating a salad for lunch in the backyard when I got back and told him, "Ed Keck was waiting for me in the park."

Todd stopped mid-bite. "*What?*"

I told him what Ed had proposed. Again, I couldn't bring myself to mention the surprise blow job at Genesis. I saw no point, and these current developments were bad enough.

"How did he find you?"

"I don't know. He wouldn't say. But you see what he's going to do, I assume. As soon as I find the tape, he's going to have me killed. Me and God only knows who else. Maybe everybody here."

We were sitting on a rusty outdoor swing, which was squeaking, as Todd finished his salad and thought about the matter. "There's something off here," he said. "Something doesn't add up."

"What do you mean?"

"Well, why would he dredge up a tape that's probably long forgotten and gathering dust in storage somewhere, if it exists at all. It's almost like he *wants* to be exposed. Not consciously, maybe, but still..."

"You've got a point," I said. "He's so intrinsically self-loathing that he might have a subconscious urge to self-destruct."

"He wouldn't be the first."

"Then again, this could be just what he says it is: an attempt to destroy the one piece of evidence that could bring him down."

"And destroy you with it. And me too."

"I'd like to say we're being paranoid. But I don't think we are."

"Ironic," said Todd. "It's just the kind of tape we might have made of him eventually. Except now we don't have to. If it still exists."

"I know," I said. "That crossed my mind too."

"So what are you going to do?"

"Find the tape. If I can."

"And then?"

"I'm not sure. But certainly not give it to Ed."

"We could release it to the media."

"Maybe." I knew Todd wasn't going to like what I had to say next. "Look, I can't talk to Rachel over the phone about this. I'm going to have to go back to L.A."

"Figured," he said, low-key. "Where will we stay? You think that place in the Palisades is still too hot?"

"We?"

"Save your breath. I'm going with you. My ass is on the line either way. Plus I have a plastic gun that won't show up on the airport x-ray machines."

"A plastic gun?"

"Sure. Nine-millimeter. Made in Finland. Takes a 17-round clip just like a Glock. You can't rapid-fire, though. That's the only catch. If you emptied the clip all at once, the barrel would melt. Otherwise..."

I didn't argue. I didn't like the idea of putting Todd in danger. But he already was now that Ed had found me. And given what had happened on my last trip to L.A., I kind of liked the idea of having somebody watching my back.

We got a hotel room in Santa Monica, paying in cash.

"What do you think about selling the tape to the media?" Todd said as we killed time, waiting for Rachel to return home from work.

"I've thought about that."

"And?"

"I don't have a problem with it ethically, if that's what

you're asking. This isn't like some paparazzi thing with Princess Diana. This is a twisted, genocidal scumbag, potentially a 21st-century Hitler. And we have a chance to bring him down. Which I think should be the main objective. But being a saint about the whole thing won't pay the bills. I mean, why give it to Tom Brokaw when we can sell it to a tabloid show for God only knows how much. And Brokaw will end up showing it *anyway*, along with every other news outlet."

"That's pretty much my thinking too," Todd said.

"Of course, this is all academic until we find the tape. *If* we find the tape."

Todd looked at his watch. "What time did you say Rachel gets home?"

We reached Rachel's Hollywood hills cottage around 7 o'clock. Since it was summer, it was still light out. Her Saab in the driveway told us she was home.

We stepped to the door, and I rang the bell.

Rachel let us in, and I introduced her to Todd. She took us out onto the back patio and served us iced tea. We made small talk for a few minutes, and then I told her why we were there. At which point she became visibly frightened.

"Jim, I'm sorry," she said. "But I want no more involvement in this."

"I understand you're frightened," I said. "I know some men came to see you, whom I'm told were politely intimidating."

"Those men were right-wing theocratic zealots," said Todd. "With horrific plans for America. Gays in particular."

"I promise you," I said, "that you will not be further involved in any way."

"Jack Ward," she said. "I don't know his address. Somewhere in West Hollywood, I think. Now go. Please."

As Todd and I drove down through the Hollywood hills, I explained. "I vaguely remember Jack. I met him once or twice at parties in the '80s. He was Donny's boyfriend. But it was on-again, off-again. Very stormy, as I recall."

"So he might have the tape?"

"Maybe." We were coming to Sunset Boulevard. "Let's find a phone book and see if he's listed."

He was. On Dicks Street. One of the narrow residential streets in West Hollywood that often shows up in coffee-table architecture books with titles like *Kitsch L.A.* It was easy to see why. Some of the houses were as originally built—postwar stucco bungalows. But many had been redone in the '60s in the gay designer style of that period, the most notorious feature of which was the false front with a two-story "L.A. door." Greco-Roman touches were common as well—urns or plaster cupid statues framing the door or set on the corners of the false front—which often clashed with sloping French-style Mansard aluminum roofs.

Jack's place was not that noxious. Instead it was so overgrown with ivy and purple bougainvillea that you could barely see its cracked white stucco. The house reeked of neglect. And sorrow.

Stepping through the gate and walking up the short path to the front door, we heard John Lee Hooker music. It was loud, a scratchy old vinyl recording. As soon as I heard it, I knew Jack would be drunk when he opened the door, and he was. Very. We had to knock several times before he answered.

"Yeah, what?" he said, bleary-eyed.

His condition was a shock. I remembered him as a young, blond farmboy type—like the singer Bryan Adams without the acne scars. That was who he'd reminded me of in the '80s. Maybe he'd been older than he looked. Because he looked at least 60 now—fat, puffy-faced, baggy-eyed, the boy shot to hell by gallons of hard liquor. He had a tumbler of whiskey in his hand, and he stank as if he hadn't bathed in days.

"Jack," I said, aware I was speaking to a man in a blackout. "You probably don't remember me. I'm James Robert Baker, the writer. I was a friend of Donny's."

"Oh, right," he said.

I pointed to Todd. "This is my friend Reese." That was Todd's fake ID name. "We've come here all the way from Orlando, on something of a quest."

Jack took a large swallow of alcohol. "A quest?"

"Perhaps I should let Reese explain."

Aware of Jack's condition, Todd spoke carefully and clearly. "I have reason to believe that my late brother, Philip, appeared in a film, a videotape to be more exact, that your late boyfriend, Donny, shot shortly before his death. Now, here's the thing, not long after Philip's own death in 1988, our father, who was extremely homophobic, took possession of all of Philip's things, and before I could stop him he destroyed them. Everything. Including all existing photos of Philip. So those of us in the family who did love him, who still miss him, have been left all these years with nothing, save our memories. Now, we understand this tape he made with Donny is pornographic. Which, as a gay man, would not bother me. And I certainly make no judgments on his participation in such a tape, or on Donny's desire to make it. But you may see what I'm driving at, Jack. Even the most explicit tape would likely contain images of Philip fully clothed. Or at the very least, images of his face, which could be cut from other material and made into still photos for those family members with more delicate sensibilities. You see what I'm saying. This tape of Philip, if it still exists, is all we have left of him."

I added, "We understand, Jack, that the tape was never finished or released. But perhaps you have some idea—"

"What's it called?"

"The working title," said Todd, "was *After Gym Class.*"

Jack drained his glass and looked at us with difficulty. I had no idea what was coming—if he was going to throw up, yell at us, pass out, or slam the door. Finally he said, "Wait here."

He went back into the house, pausing to shut off the music—predictably scraping the needle across the record as he did. In a minute he reeled back with some keys in one hand. "C'mon," he said. "It's about a block from here." He started out the door, then stopped. "Wait. Almost forgot." He went back into the house and returned with a flashlight. He tested it. It worked, barely.

"C'mon," he said as he staggered out the door and down the

walk. "I got some stuff in storage. In a garage in the next block."

Todd and I followed as Jack explained. "Donny's father was an asshole too. So I know where you guys are at. He destroyed a bunch of Donny's stuff. He did the same evil shit. He came in and took Donny's stuff and then burned it. Fucking right-wing piece of shit."

We turned the corner, and Jack led us up a dark, narrow alley. "Then these scumbags came around. I think they were Mafia. They all had Italian names. They wanted Donny's stuff too. I said, 'Fuck you. He's dead. His dad destroyed his stuff. So fuck you too.' But I saved a lot of it. It's up here in the garage. Once—" He stopped. "Fuck. Which one is it?" There was a row of garages. "Once about five years ago— There it is. That's it." He walked to the garage, dug out his keys, and began trying each in the padlock. "Once about five years ago I tried to look at some of this. Sort through it. But I started crying. I watched a tape of Donny and me. At the beach. And I started crying. He was so fucking beautiful."

He started crying again now.

I said, "Jack, why don't you let me do that?"

He handed me the keys and flashlight. I gave the flashlight to Todd, who shined it on the padlock. In a moment I found the right key and the lock snapped open.

I lifted the garage door and Todd shined the light inside. It was a mess, filled with old furniture, cardboard boxes, and black plastic boxes of videotapes—both VHS and ¾-inch. Two of the ¾-inch Sony tapes were labeled "Gym Class Rough Cut" and "Gym Class Outtakes."

"Jack," I said, "I think these are what we need."

"Take them," he said. "I don't care. Just take them."

"Can we help you back to the house?" Todd asked.

"Just go. I'll stay here."

By the time we left with the tapes, it was nearing midnight. We were eager to see what was on them, but to do that we needed a ¾-inch playback deck—as opposed to a common VHS VCR. I knew of a small editing house in West Hollywood that had that equipment, but it wouldn't be open until morning. There was one other immediate option: Phil had ¾-inch decks in the Vault.

We decided to chance it.

We parked several blocks away and went in through the back gate, in case the house was being watched.

Once inside, we felt secure. There were lights burning on automatic timers, but we didn't turn on any new ones. We got sodas from the kitchen and went straight to the editing room in the basement, where there were no windows. There we did turn on the lights, and then we stuck the rough-cut tape into the deck.

It didn't take long to see that we'd found what we'd been looking for. There was a skinny young Ed Keck, his brown hair much longer and floppier than now. He entered the locker room in gym clothes—blue trunks, white T-shirt, athletic shoes and socks—along with another young man, a blond hayseed type. For a moment I thought it might be Jack, but it wasn't. The young men began to take off their clothes. The picture cut to a close-up of Ed's crotch as he pulled down his jockstrap, and the small cock I'd seen at Genesis flopped out. He'd clearly been cast on the basis of his boyishness and not his dick size.

In a moment the coach came in. He was also wearing shorts, but no shirt. Thick, dark hair densely covered his chest and stomach. The hair on his head was Marine Corps short. His features were hyperbutch, reminding me a lot of the actor Ed Harris. He had a paddle in his hand.

With typically bad dialogue and acting, the coach chastised the two "boys" for messing up a game. It wasn't clear what sport they'd been playing, only that they'd done it poorly. "I'm sorry, Coach," Ed said flatly, though even here I would have recognized his voice with my eyes closed. His eyes were glassy, as if he were tweaked.

In a great piece of dialogue that might have come from a Howard Hawks film—if, for example, the homoeroticism in *Red River* had been explicit—the coach grabbed Ed's face and said, "Sorry's not enough, mister. And words are cheap. A real man shows he's sorry by suckin' some cock."

So that's what Ed did—Ed and the blond kid. The coach pushed them both to their knees, whipped out his fat hard rod, and had them both work it: licking it up and down either side, mouthing the shiny head, tonguing his egg-size balls.

Todd and I exchanged looks.

"I see why he's concerned," Todd said dryly. "If Christians were upset by Pat Boone's heavy metal album, they're gonna shit bricks when they see this. Even pixilated."

And so it went. Ed sucked the blond kid's cock for a while. Then, in a close-up, Ed spread the coach's hairy butt cheeks and licked his butch hole. The blond kid did the same to Ed's little pink bunger. Then, while Ed sucked the blond kid's cock, the coach fucked him. Hard. Ed winced, and it didn't look like he was acting.

Through it all, Ed's cock never got hard. Likely because he was, as he'd told me, on speed, which often leads to impotence.

To be honest, my feelings about porn in general are extremely ambivalent. I can't say I haven't seen stuff I find hot, but too often there's a subtext of exploitation. And that definitely was the case here. With Ed especially. You could see that he was strung out and desperate and selling his body for chump change.

Todd was having the same reaction. "This is sad."

"I know."

"Don't misunderstand me. I'm not losing my nerve or anything. But it's just very, very sad that anyone would fall so low."

Then the phone rang. Not my cell phone, which wasn't turned on, but Phil's land line. It scared the shit out of both of us. Obviously, we didn't even consider picking up. We did, however, run upstairs to the kitchen, where Phil kept his answering machine, to see if the caller would leave a message.

He did. And he spoke directly to me. "Jim, this is Ed." He sounded extremely upset. "I'm calling you, hoping you'll get this. I left a message in Madison too, and I tried your cell phone. I just want you to know that the tape doesn't matter anymore. I was at a...at a rest stop. A rest stop in Virginia. And...and I...I came on to a vice cop. So the tape doesn't matter anymore."

I started to pick up, but Todd pushed my hand aside. "It could be a trick!"

"I've hurt so many people," he said. "And Bud will never forgive me. So I'm going to meet Jesus."

I brushed Todd's hand aside and picked up, but it was too late. "Ed?" Nothing. Then a dial tone.

"You think that was for real?" Todd said.

"Maybe," I said. "It sure sounded real."

"I guess we should keep an eye on the news."

We didn't have to wait long to find out what happened to Ed. We spent the night in the Vault, and the next morning we turned on CNN.

Ed had been in Washington, D.C., in his apartment at the Watergate. From the balcony he'd jumped seven stories to his death. They showed a shot of his sheet-covered body on a patio. One side of the sheet was red with blood.

He'd left a suicide note, portions of which they showed onscreen. It read much the same as his phone message to me.

He had been arrested for lewd conduct at a rest stop near Langley, Va. As he'd said on the phone, he had apparently made an overture to an undercover vice cop. He'd only been in jail a few hours before being released on his own recognizance. But Bud Chaswell had been alerted. And so had the media. There'd been a meeting between Ed and Bud, the nature of which was not hard to imagine. Ed had been the heir apparent to Bud's religious and political empire, a cornerstone of which had been Bud's intense and unrelenting homophobia. Ed's arrest would not have been something Bud could accept. So it's safe to assume Ed was relieved of the presidency of the Christian Family Alliance on the spot. It's safe to also assume that Ed saw his dream of becoming president swirling down the toilet.

Bud never got the chance to announce Ed's "resignation," as he termed it in the statement he made after Ed's death. "We are very saddened by this tragic event," he told the packed press conference at his compound in North Carolina. "It's no secret that Ed was like a son to me." His squinty blue eyes brimmed with tears. "As for this aspect of his personal life, I had no clue. Honestly," said Bud, "I can't help but wonder if Satan didn't set him up as a special target, knowing how much Ed had to give to the world in Jesus' name. Satan tempted Jesus too. But Jesus Christ was divine. While Ed Keck was, after all, only a man." He waved away a flurry of questions as he appeared to break down in tears and a young aide led him away from the podium.

Were the tears real? Possibly. But I'm certain Bud was glad Ed had made a quick exit. It gave Bud a chance to turn Ed into a martyr with his later allegation that "an extensive investigation" had "proved" that Ed did nothing, that he was framed. Framed and forced to write a suicide note before he was pushed from the Watergate window. By homosexual zealots, of course.

After about 30 minutes, Todd turned off the TV. We took our coffee onto the second-floor terrace and sat quietly in the bright sunlight for several minutes. Finally, Todd said, "I can see why people like it here. You hear so many horror stories about L.A., but this is very pleasant."

"Yes, it is. Of course, this isn't South Central or East L.A. Or even Downey. I've always felt that's what really killed Karen Carpenter. She never got out of Downey."

"Where's Downey?"

Before I could answer, an object thrown from below smacked the tile floor of the terrace a few feet from where we were sitting. I reeled when I saw what it was. Todd did more than that. He said, "Oh, God, God, God!" And then he doubled over in his chair and puked.

I ducked over to check it out more closely, to be certain what it was—or rather *who* it was. And a closer look confirmed that it was in fact Steve's severed head. His eyes were closed, thank God. His skin had not yet lost its normal healthy tone, indicating that his decapitation was recent. Todd was still vomiting violently, but for some reason I was too stunned to get sick. It was so horrendous and unexpected that I'd gone into a protective numbed-out mode.

There was a rolled up note sticking out of Steve's mouth, clearly meant to be found and read. I pulled it out and opened it. And that's when I really got upset. It read: "Call *Mutti.*"

"Oh, fuck," I said. "I hope this isn't what I think it is. I hope this is just a sick joke."

"Joke?" Todd said. *"Joke?* It's somebody's head! What kind of joke is that?"

"No, I mean *this."* I handed him the note.

By now, Todd had puked everything there was to puke. He was pale and shaking, but calmer. *"Mutti?"*

"German for 'mother.' "

"What does that mean?" Cringing, Todd looked at Steve's head. "And who is that? What the fuck is going on?"

I told him the head was Steve's, reminding him who Steve

was. Then I went inside to call my mother. But before I could pick up the phone to dial her number, it rang. I picked up, figuring whoever it was already knew I was there. "Yes?"

"James. I am not certain if you find our note." He had a heavy German accent. "Do you know we are at your mother's?"

"Yes, I know. I found the note. Who is this?"

"Let us not waste time," he said. "I think if you recall your last trip to Berlin, that will answer your question. No?"

I'd all but forgotten about Baldur Schenk. I mean, I knew his people might be after me. But with all the other people trying to kill me... Maybe I'd been hoping that with Baldur dead, his Fourth Reich shtick would crumble and his followers would be too demoralized to organize a search for me.

"You were not easy to locate, James," he said. "Until we find your Christian friend who is now without his head."

"Look, you might not believe me, but what happened with Baldur was truly an accident."

"This is what your friend told us as well. But we can never know for sure without being inside your brain. And that is not why we are here with your mother now. We are here because your friend Steve also told us about the computer program. The Revelations program."

"That doesn't exist," I said. "It was destroyed in Tennessee."

"Then your mother will be destroyed in Santa Barbara."

My mother did live in Santa Barbara. Which meant they'd definitely located her.

"Listen to me, James. We are here with your *mutti*, and you have two hours to bring us this Revelations. Do you understand?"

"I think so."

"We want the Revelations, James. Or she will be like your old boyfriend. It is now almost 1 o'clock. We give you until 3 o'clock. If you arrive late, you will be quite reminded of the actress Diane Rainey. We have a sharp saw. Your *mutti* has a microwave. We have been much inspired by our Russian counterparts. Bring the software now, James. And let us hope you don't get caught in a traffic jam. Unless you have a recipe for *mutti kopf,* hmm? *Auf wiedersehen."*

As a rule, it takes two hours to reach Santa Barbara from the Palisades. You can make it in less if you haul ass.

"Let's go," I yelled at Todd. "I'll explain on the way."

"Wait," said Todd. Despite being freaked out, he was not without foresight. "Do we need guns? All we have is the plastic one."

"You're right."

We broke into Phil's glass gun case downstairs and took a shotgun, a Glock, a .357 Colt Python, and ammunition. Then I grabbed three CD-ROMs at random: Cinemania '98, Adobe Acrobat, and a Windows upgrade disk. In case I needed to pretend I actually had Revelations with me.

By the time we actually got on the road, it was after 1 o'clock. From our location in the Palisades, we had a choice of two routes north to Santa Barbara. We could take the Ventura Freeway, or we could go back to PCH and take that up through Oxnard. A tough call. The freeway would be faster—unless it was jammed. And the Ventura through the Valley was often jammed. That's why I opted for PCH.

As I roared down Sunset Boulevard through a well-known speed-trap area, Todd said, "OK, fill me in."

I did.

He said, "I guess it's not surprising they'd find you eventually."

"I guess not."

"So what's your mom like?"

"She's cool. I mean, she *looks* conventional. Not unlike June Cleaver. Like a 65-year-old June Cleaver. But politically she's extremely left-wing. I mean, she actually left the country during Vietnam. Lived in Canada, she was so disgusted with things here. And she's read all my books. Even the craziest parts don't faze her. In fact, I think she's where I got my sense of humor."

"Jeez," Todd said. "I could never show my mother your books. She'd have a stroke by page 10."

"Well, my mom's an anomaly in a lot of ways. I love her dearly. And I *don't* want to see her head spinning in a microwave."

"So what are we going to do when we get there?"

"I don't know. I'm still thinking. It'll depend on the situation. On how many of them there are. How do you feel about killing?"

I'd already given him the Glock. He told me he'd trained on semiautomatic weapons. And I figured I could better handle the Python's recoil—thanks to my early pistol-range practice with my gun nut father.

"Well, I've never done that," he said.

"I know. That's why I ask. But we may need to here. It could well come down to that."

"They're neo-Nazis, right?"

"Yes."

"That makes it easier. I'll pretend it's a movie."

"Don't pretend too much. This is real. It's not squibs and blanks."

I was pushing 80 through Malibu. I'd decided it was worth it. Even if we got a ticket, we'd probably still come out ahead.

Then, in a desolate stretch of highway south of Point Mugu, where there's nothing but barren red rock cliffs on one side and a skimpy beach on the other, I realized we were being followed.

"Don't look back," I said. "But a shit-brown Dodge has been on our tail since Trancas. At least that's where I first noticed it."

"Are you sure?"

"They're matching our speed. And a few minutes ago I slowed down and they did too."

Todd started to turn around.

"*Don't* look back!"

"Who do you think it is?"

"It might be the Germans who tossed the head. But they wouldn't need to tail us since they know where we're going. It might be the Russians. The car *is* pretty ugly. But I doubt it. They've probably written me off. So it's probably Genesis."

"You think they followed Steve?"

"Well, his head maybe."

"Doesn't really matter, does it?"

"Who it is? Or how they found us?"

"Either."

He had a point.

"If it's Genesis," I said, "they don't know where we're headed. I'll try to lose them when we get closer to Santa Barbara. If we have time."

We were fast approaching Oxnard, where there was a series of stoplights before we connected to the 101 freeway that would take us through Ventura. As the first light came up, the Dodge receded in the rearview mirror. Whoever it was clearly didn't want to end up right behind us, where we could get a good look at them.

"You know," said Todd. "even if it is Genesis, they might know where we're going. I mean, if the Nazis found your mother, Genesis probably could too."

"Possibly," I said, not wanting to think about it but doing so anyway. "Probably, actually. They don't seem too concerned about losing us." The Dodge had dropped a full stoplight behind.

There was nothing to do but keep the pedal to the floor. Amazingly, we weren't stopped for speeding, even though I was doing 90 through Ventura and we passed another car that *had* been stopped. The motorcycle cop glared at us. I figured he might be on our ass once he was done. But it didn't happen.

As we roared through Montecito, the southern suburb of Santa Barbara, we had 25 minutes before the 3 o'clock deadline. So I got off the freeway at Milpas, which was still some distance from my mother's. Then I did some fast zigzags through the side streets of the dumpy part of town, until a few blocks south of State Street, Santa Barbara's main drag, I said to Todd, "I think we lost them."

Indeed, there was no sign of the Dodge, and there hadn't been for a number of turns, though they had followed us off the freeway at Milpas.

"Let's hope they *stay* lost," Todd said. "How much farther?"

"She's on the next street after this," I said as we came to a red light at State Street. "And a few blocks north. In a duplex."

The light took forever to change. State Street itself, in the downtown area, was crowded with traffic and pedestrians. Within the last decade or so, it had been renovated, yuppified. So there were lots of people out—families, couples, students out strolling, shopping, and sitting at sidewalk cafés.

Finally the light changed. Within a few minutes we were on a shady residential street, approaching my mother's Spanish-style duplex. Even from a distance, I could see the living room picture window undraped, which surprised me.

"I'll tell you what," I said. "I'd like you to walk down the street. I'd do it myself, but they'd recognize me. You can walk on the other side of the street and still see in the window. It will no doubt look innocent, or they would've drawn the drapes. You'll probably see my mom sitting there with several men. I want to know how many, where she's sitting, and where the men are. Can you do that?"

He looked scared but said, "Yeah."

"All right. In a minute I'll drive around the block and pick you up at the other end."

He opened the passenger door. He was going to do it, but he looked sick with fear.

"Todd, even on the off chance that they know what you look like too, they're not going to do anything to attract attention. Not when they think I'm bringing them what they want." I indicated the CD-ROMs on the seat.

"I know," he said. "I already thought of that." He got out and started up the sidewalk.

I can't say I wasn't worried. I didn't know if they'd recognize Todd, but at the very least they'd be suspicious. Still, I couldn't imagine they'd open fire on him out in the open—since that would bring the police and blow their plan. But who the fuck knew?

I waited and watched. His walking was a little jerky, but his look through the window was nicely executed. He appeared to shift his eyes without turning his head. Once he was past the danger point, I whipped around the block to meet him.

Todd looked puzzled as he climbed back into the car.

"So?"

"I don't know," he said. "I saw your mom all right."

"And?"

"She was sitting on the sofa next to this old guy. This old guy with a white flattop. He looked like you, Jim. Like you in 30 years. He was holding your mother's hand, and they were talking. She didn't look scared at all. And there was nobody else there."

I was more than blown away. "You looked in the unit on the right?"

"Yes."

"And you could see the whole living room?"

"Plain as day."

"And there was nobody there but my mom and this guy?"

"Unless the rest of the Germans were hiding in the bathroom or something. But your mom didn't look even remotely upset. On the contrary. She was cuddling up with this guy. Who really does look like you."

And then it hit me. "You're describing *my father.* He still has a lame '50s flattop."

"I'm just telling you what I saw. I thought your parents—"

"They *are* divorced," I said. "For about 20 years."

"I don't get it."

"The Germans are in the wrong duplex. They've got Mrs. Henderson. Who also has a son named Jim. My mother's last name is *Anderson.* They fucked up."

"You can't be serious."

Before I could answer, I saw my parents drive past in a pale blue Buick Regal, my father at the wheel. I hadn't seen my father in almost 15 years, so just seeing him was a jolt. Let alone back with my mother.

I pulled out and followed them.

"What's going on?" Todd said.

"That's my mom and dad. In the Buick."

"Well where the hell are they going?"

I handed him my cell phone. "I don't have the slightest fucking clue where they're going. But Mrs. Henderson is pissing in her Depends right now. Call 911."

I kept focused on my father's Buick, following it through a green light across State Street. And I kept an eye on the rearview mirror as well, for the Germans or whoever was in the shit-brown Dodge. But nobody appeared to be following us.

As Todd explained to a befuddled 911 operator that they needed to rescue Mrs. Henderson but fast, I realized where my dad was going: the old Santa Barbara Mission. That would be romantic. Very unlike my father, but a good ploy if he was trying to get back together with Mom.

Within a few minutes the Buick pulled into the mission parking lot. As usual, the grounds were strewn with tourists. The mission itself was not all that impressive. Fairly plain as Spanish missions go. A crude, unadorned whitewashed chapel and a long building running over to one side with a porch and a gift shop. There were also gardens and other buildings you couldn't see from the front. A line of people stood by the gift shop, waiting for a tour to begin.

My mom and dad were getting out of his car when I pulled up beside them. When my mom saw me she jumped. My dad's jaw dropped.

"Jim!" my mom said. "What are you doing here?"

"Good question, Doris," my dad said. His gruff voice brought back a lot of foul memories. It might have been 15 years since I'd last heard it, but it was the same voice I'd heard at *age* 15.

"No time to explain. Mom, what's Mrs. Henderson's number?" It had just occurred to me that the police might be slow in responding or that they might have thought Todd's call was a crank and that I might be able to save her life by calling and telling the Germans about their mistake.

"Vera?"

"Right. Vera. Your next-door neighbor. The number!"

"I don't know it, honey," my mom said. "It's on my speed dial at home. Why do you want to call Vera?"

"So her head won't end up in her microwave." I was already punching Information on my cell phone.

"What on earth—" my mom began.

"Mom, there isn't time. Say hello to Todd. He's my boyfriend. Todd, the old guy's my right-wing asshole dad."

"All right, mister." My dad did his scowling shtick. "Watch that talk."

"Look," I said calmly while the phone was ringing, "I'm trying to do a good deed here. So just shut the fuck up, Dad."

My mom touched my father's arm and looked at him as if to tell him she concurred with me.

I got information and had it automatically dial Vera's number.

The German guy answered. "Hello?"

"Hi. It's me. How you guys doing?"

"*James.* We are anxious. You are late."

"Well, look. Here's the deal. Listen closely. You fucked up. The woman you're holding is *not* my mother. You went to the wrong half of the duplex. Understand? My mom lives next door and she's with me now. You've got Mrs. *Henderson,* who also has a son named Jim. My mother's name is *Anderson.*"

"Oh, James," he said. "This is quite distressing."

"I'm sure it is. But if you ask her—"

"I can do that," he said. "But I do not think she will respond. Not with her head going around in circles and stinking up this place."

I felt punched. "Oh, God. Tell me you're bluffing."

"James, truly I believe you. But I am not bluffing. When you don't show up, we think you are not coming. So..."

"*Fuck.*"

I slammed down the phone.

"Shit," said Todd.

I leaned against my dad's hot car for a moment, too blown out to move. I guess I kind of spaced out for a while—until I heard my father hustling around to the trunk of the car, unlocking it. And Todd said, "Jim, they've got your mom!"

I knew who he meant before I even saw them: the people in the Dodge. They'd somehow followed us to the mission. And they were Genesis people, as we'd predicted. I recognized the one who'd grabbed my mom, who was pulling her toward the chapel steps.

It was Gene, the blob who'd kept the porno library in Tennessee.

Covering for Gene were two younger Genesis bots, both of whom had drawn guns. Gene was unarmed, or so it seemed. He was, inexplicably, holding a foot-long plastic Jesus statuette under my mother's chin. As if it were a weapon of some sort.

Gene dragged my mother up to the aged wooden chapel doors. And when he found them locked, he was clearly upset. He seemed uncertain as to what to do next.

"Hey, Gene," I called, "long time no see. What's with the plastic Jesus? You got a gun in it?"

"It's much more than that, heathen," Gene said.

Peripherally I saw what my dad was up to. He'd taken a .45 semiautomatic from his trunk.

"Dad, chill," I said. "I mean it."

My mother was stiff with fear, shut down, her expression gone blank.

"This is no ordinary Jesus," Gene said.

"I can see that. It's much tackier than most. In fact, it's almost as tacky as those Chuck Heston Bible flicks you love so—"

"I'm holding a biological weapon," Gene announced.

"You only do that when you're beating off."

"This is not a joke. This statuette is filled with Apocola. It's based on the Ebola virus, only it's much, much more dangerous. We developed it in our lab."

"No shit?" I was certain he was bluffing. "And I thought you were researching bad haircuts and cellulite in there. Or trying to whip up a non-Satanic version of Mountain Dew. I recall some talk of Jesus Juice." That last bit was true. I had heard talk of that while I was there. And what Gene said next made me wish I hadn't.

"That's what *this* is," he said. He had a look in his eye that's hard to describe. A little like Slim Pickens riding the nuclear bomb in *Dr. Strangelove.* "This statue is made of plastic," he said. "It won't take much to crack it. And if it cracks, the virus will be released into the air. It's airborne and self-replicates, and there's no antidote. It will kill us all in seconds. Everyone here at the mission. Then it will spread across the city. In less than an hour Santa Barbara will be wiped out. And it won't stop there. The wind will carry it as it continues to replicate. Las Vegas, Denver, Chicago, New York. Or it might go the other way. Hawaii, Japan. No matter. Whichever way the wind blows, life as we know it will end."

"What about you?" I said.

"Everyone and everything. I have no fear. For this is the mighty will of God."

"Horseshit," said my dad. He was still holding his .45.

I took a quick look at the armed bots and saw their weapons were similar. They were both in their early 20s, clean-cut, plain-faced.

"Give us back Revelations," said Gene, "and save the world. Or keep it and die and burn in eternal hell with all the other sinners."

I leaned back against the car and crossed my arms. "I don't believe you, Gene. I'm calling your bluff."

I'd planned to say more, but it was here that my father, with typically bad timing, opened fire. His first bullet struck one of the young bots in the chest. The other bot returned fire as my father kept shooting.

I felt a sting in my chest and looked down and saw blood. Then a searing pain in my sternum, very close to my heart. I recall thinking, *Oh, fuck, this is it. I'm going.* Then I collapsed and blacked out.

You can make what you will of what follows. I'm simply reporting what I remember. I'm not saying any of this is true—at least not in the conventional sense, as we normally experience truth. That said, this is what happened.

I woke up not on the asphalt of the mission parking lot, or in an ambulance, or a hospital recovery room, or even my home. I woke up on an escalator, the kind you'd find in a department store, heading up

I pulled myself up and saw the wound in my chest, though it was no longer bleeding. Then I saw where the escalator was. It was in the clouds. It was taking me up through layers of fluffy white clouds. I looked down and saw the escalator descending for what looked like miles. Very far below, I could see its starting point: the planet Earth, about the size of a full moon. I looked up ahead: The clouds were so thick that I couldn't see where the escalator was taking me. Although it wasn't hard to guess.

I had a sense of being fully conscious, and everything looked quite real. So much so that I almost panicked, since I do have a certain fear of heights. But I got a grip on myself—

or, more precisely, a grip on the escalator's rubber handrails—and assured myself that I'd be safe as long as I stayed where I was and went along for the ride. I also noticed that the escalator was old, its steel corroded. The handrails were weathered and cracked. The mechanism squeaked. None of which was reassuring in any way.

Several minutes passed as I moved higher and deeper into the clouds, to the point where the earth was no longer visible. Guessing this was taking me to heaven, I had some concern about what might await me. This seemed like such a warped Christian view of the place that I wondered exactly how I'd be welcomed, if they might check me out and spring a trapdoor to hell. I mean, I wondered if all the hokey shit about harps and singing and whatever else might be true, and if so, if maybe I didn't want to turn around and scramble down the upward-moving stairs. Given the distance, though, that didn't seem viable. I had no choice but to wait and see where I was going.

I had my answer soon enough. Looking through a break in the clouds, I saw a woman dressed in white waiting for me at a landing. The landing itself was dilapidated: chipped, weathered arches of a Greco-Roman design. The woman's robes were long and flowing and smacked of some sort of religious cult. I wondered if I'd somehow been sent to the Genesis version of heaven.

Then, as I approached the landing, I saw the woman's face and felt great relief, followed by astonishment and confusion. She was, or at least she appeared to be, the stunning French film star Catherine Deneuve.

"Careful," she said, as the escalator ended at the landing

and I stepped off onto a dirty marble floor. Her accent and voice were also Deneuve's. For all practical purposes, she *was* Deneuve.

"How are you feeling?" she asked.

"What do you mean?"

"Your wound no longer hurts?"

I touched my chest. "No."

"Good. We made it stop. Otherwise it would be quite painful."

By now I'd cased the landing. We were alone, and there was a set of double doors, again Greco-Roman, in a high, cracked plaster wall.

"Could you please tell me what's going on?" I said. "Is this a dream?"

"It is not a dream, James."

"Then why do you look like Catherine Deneuve? Or are you really her?"

"The answer is both yes and no," she said. "My living self remains on Earth. But I am she in the future. Do you understand?"

"No."

"It has to do with time and space. I could speak of it more, but there's no...time. We have brought you here in a special way, James. Because we need you to help us."

"Help you? In what way?"

She touched one of the two ornate brass doorknobs. "This is a secret entrance. The back door to heaven. Things are not good here. We have a big problem." She paused. "I must tell you this now, James. I appear to you as Catherine Deneuve, which is not a falsehood, for I am truly Catherine Deneuve in the future. But in the past, in the time of Christ, I was known as Mary Magdalene."

"Hold on," I said. "You're Catherine Deneuve in the future and Mary Magdalene in the past? So who are you now?"

"I understand your skepticism. You would make a Shirley MacLaine joke, were it not too dated. But please put aside your cynicism. We need your help now. The stakes could not be more high."

"OK," I said. "But I don't understand what the fuck is going on here. Pardon my French. Heh. No pun intended. So shoot."

"How do I put this...?" She gently touched my hand and spoke in a soft voice. "God is...insane. He has been from the start. Going back to the beginning, he was always a sadist. You can see this in the Bible. In the Old Testament."

"I've noticed."

"But now he is old, very old, and he has become *quite* demented. He still has the power of God, though, so everyone fears him. No one will stop him, even though what he does gets worse all the time. But you have shown courage. I think you may be our last hope." She paused to emphasize what followed. "God plans to destroy all the life he controls. If he is not stopped soon, he will do it."

She seemed sincere in her urgency.

"OK," I said. "That's interesting. But let me ask you: Where does Jesus figure in? I'm assuming you believe in Jesus if you claim to be Mary Magdalene."

"Indeed," she said. "I was coming to that. The truth is quite different from what most on Earth think. The Christians especially have things very wrong. In fact, Christ was always at odds with God, his father. He went down to

Earth to try to undo the damage God had caused. He brought a new word meant to replace the old. This is clear to some, but ignored by many.

"When God discovered what Christ was doing, he became quite angry. Hence the Crucifixion. A very painful way to die. A punishment. There is much more I could tell you, but there is no time. *This* is what you need to know: Jesus did not rise again. That is Christian myth. In truth, God gave him an excruciating death and brought him back here. And since that time, Christ has been imprisoned by his father. This is why he cannot return to earth. This is why he cannot object to the many vile things done in his name. He knows of these things. There are ways we can reach him. But he can do nothing—except seethe with anger that he is unable to stop the evil that men do in his name."

"You're telling me Christ is in *jail*?"

"Yes." Her voice grew more urgent. "Once God is dead, we can free Christ. God is like Hitler. Do you understand? In fact, he is much worse. But if God is killed, it will be as it was with the Third Reich on Earth. With God dead, the current structure of heaven will crumble. Believe me," she said, "there are many who yearn as I do for Christ's release. For once he is free, all will be different. God is sadistic, cruel, deranged. Christ embodies love, compassion, forgiveness. Do you see?"

"Yeah, I mean, I understand what you're saying. But I'm not sure I buy that *this* is really happening. I mean, this conversation with you right now. I recall being shot. I think I may be dreaming or hallucinating."

"James..." She reached for my hand, and I felt the soft warmth of her touch. "You are not dreaming. You are standing with me at the back door to heaven. And only you can stop God. And in so doing save the earth and many other worlds from great pain and suffering."

"Other worlds?"

"The universe is infinite. Within it there are many gods. But our God controls the earth and 10,000 other worlds."

"*Ten thousand?*"

"Please, James. Later I can tell you much more of these matters. But right now God must be killed. And you must do it."

At this point, I'd decided this was all unreal. So I saw no harm or danger in playing along, any more than you'd be afraid of what happened in a dream—if you knew you were dreaming.

"OK," I said. "So how am I supposed to kill God?"

"It's simple. First you need to get close to him. We have a disguise to help you with that. Once you are inside his room, it will be easy. All you need to do is pull out the tube that feeds souls into his heart. When you do this, he will die instantly. And you will see him decay as you would a vampire in a horror film."

"A tube that feeds him souls?"

"It is just as it sounds."

"And then he'll turn to dust, like you at the end of *The Hunger?*"

"Yes, like that. God is a recluse, an invalid. He has been for many centuries. He leaves his room, his bed, only with great effort and assistance, and only rarely. He has a tube implanted here." She touched her chest. "Like...what is the term? A cath..."

"A catheter?"

"Yes. That's it. It is made of transparent material, much like plastic. It feeds him the souls of those who die in pain. This is what he lives on. This and this alone. But you will see only a flow of translucent bubbles moving through the tube, since the soul is essentially invisible. Each bubble encases a soul. These souls are crucial to his survival. He needs this steady stream. If it is severed, even briefly, his existence will end."

"So you're asking me to play God with God?"

She didn't smile. She just said, "Yes."

"OK. So how do I get in to see him? I mean, what's this disguise thing?"

"God likes to watch Earth's TV. He enjoys the cheap shows, such as *Sea Crew.* We can make you appear as Patti Grant."

"You want me to go in drag?"

"No. We can transform you into her much more convincingly."

"So...let me get this straight. You can turn me into Patti Grant? Temporarily, right? Not permanently?"

"Precisely. Once the job is done, you can return to who you are. Or someone else, if you prefer."

"Tempting," I said. "But I'll stick with who I am. I'm used to me and I kind of like me and I have a boyfriend and all. I *can* go back? I mean, I wasn't really ready to die just yet."

"Yes. Right now, back on earth, your physical body is in an emergency room. The doctors are working on you frantically. They don't think you're going to make it. But we can see to it that you will."

"Speaking of Earth, what happened back there? Can you tell me if my mom and dad and boyfriend are all right?"

"They are all fine. The man Gene with the plastic Jesus is dead. As are the two men who were with him."

"Was there really a virus in that thing? Or was that bullshit?"

"The plastic Jesus contained nothing. It was hollow, but empty. But Gene did not know that. He thought it did contain the virus."

"That's good news. I was *pretty* sure he was bluffing, but—"

"Please," she said. "We must begin." She led me through the doors. "I will take you to the place where you will be transformed."

"Wait," I said. "It won't work. Patti Grant is dead."

"Yes. God knows of this. He saw it on TV, and he put in a special order to have her brought before him, since he finds her silicone body enticing. But his order was intercepted by our spies. Contrary to myth, God is *not* all-knowing. In fact, he consumed Patti Grant's soul long ago, but he doesn't know this. He is angry that she still has not appeared. So you see? He will be expecting you."

"Come," she said, leading me through a small, run-down foyer.

"One last question. What happens if God smells a rat? I mean, what can he do to me?"

She touched her lips with her fingers, measuring her words. "I wish you had not asked that. He could do many things, all of which are too unspeakable to dwell upon. Things that would make burning in agony in the Christian hell for all eternity seem appealing."

"That's not what I wanted to hear."

"I know," she said. "But I would not lie to you about something like that. I assure you, though, the risk is minimal. God is so far gone right now that I feel I can tell you with complete certainty that he will not catch on. When he sees you as Patti Grant, he will be smitten. You will have her body, her voice.

If you move fast and pull the tube, there can be no problem."

"But he must have guards or attendants or whatever."

"He does. Which is why I or another who is known to them cannot do this. We would be recognized, even disguised as Patti Grant. But you they do not know, so they will believe you are who you appear to be."

"And after I pull the tube, what will they do? Just let me go?"

"They will die. All those in his circle are of the same kind as him. They survive from his energy, which is why they protect him, even when they know he is insane. You will step over what remains of them as you leave God's mansion."

"God's *mansion*?"

"Yes. God lives in a garish house on a hill. It is much like Graceland. You will see."

She crossed the foyer to another set of double doors, which she threw open to reveal an astonishing vista of rolling, deep-green hills adorned with clusters of trees, British-style cottages here and there, and a winding country road. A mist laced the hills in the distance. The landscape was both real and unreal—a fairy-tale setting.

A 19th-century carriage awaited us, with a shadowy capped coachman, whose face I never did see, and four beautiful white horses. Deneuve opened the carriage door and said, "Come. It is not far to the place where you will change."

Indeed, no sooner than the two of us were inside the coach, in a kind of cinematic dissolve, we arrived at a thatched-roof cottage. A bearded man in flowing, biblical-looking robes waited for us in the open doorway.

"Hello," he said pleasantly. "I'm Peter." He extended his hand.

"I'm Jim."

"Yes. We know."

As Deneuve and I stepped into the cottage, I saw who Peter meant by *we*. Two other men in similar biblical attire. Peter introduced them to me. "This is Luke. And this is Judas."

I shook hands with both men. Luke struck me as shy and self-effacing. Judas, on the other hand, had a glint in his eyes, an air of intensity. "Don't believe what you've heard about me," he said. "It was *not* the way you think."

Peter explained. "God made us betray Christ. He worked us like puppets. In those days he could make you do anything. Put any words he wanted into your mouth."

"Jesus knows this," Judas said. "He's always known what happened. On Earth, people don't. I know I have a very bad name on Earth."

"This is true," I said.

Deneuve spoke up. "I know James would love to hear the true version of the Crucifixion. But this is neither the time nor place. I have spoken to him of our problem, and he has agreed to do what must be done."

"Then you know about the Patti Grant disguise?" Luke said.

"Yeah. I'm game. I guess. As long as it's not permanent. I really hope you're not blowing smoke up my ass about that part."

"I know this expression," Judas said. "And we are not doing that. We simply want this madness to end. We want Christ set free."

"We should get started," Peter said. "God's expecting Patti Grant today. If she doesn't show up soon, he might order a trace and discover that he's already eaten her soul."

Luke beckoned me toward the next room. "Come, James. The change is effected through use of a shower."

I followed Luke through a bedroom and into a small bathroom with a tub that had a shower faucet and a faded shower curtain with a fish design. He closed the door behind us.

"If you'd get undressed now," he said. "There's nothing to fear. This shower runs a special water. It won't hurt you, but you will feel a tingling sensation as your body transmutes into Patti Grant's."

I began to take off my clothes, though not without apprehension. "What's in the water?"

"You'd rather not know."

"Oh?"

"It would upset you. But I assure you, it won't hurt you. I think we should leave it at that."

"Maybe you're right," I said.

I was down to my boxers. I peeled those off as well.

Luke turned on the shower and adjusted the temperature. "Is this OK?"

I held my hand under the water: comfortably warm. "Yeah, it's fine."

"All right then. Please step in."

I was about to do that when I looked at my hand, the one I'd just gotten wet and which was now tingling. And it was no longer *my* hand. As I watched, it shrank and changed form, becoming much smaller, softer, feminine. Until it was Patti Grant's hand, the nails long and bright red and glossy with polish. This shook me.

"Whoa."

"James, please. It's all right. It will be a shock to see yourself as Patti Grant. But we *will* return you to your original self. It is as simple as taking another shower."

My heart was pounding, but I stepped into the tub and under the warm spray.

Immediately, as the water washed over my body, I tingled all over. And even though I knew what to expect, when I looked down at my chest and watched Patti Grant's breasts sprout from own pectorals, it was a shocker. Her perfect silicone breasts were morphing out of my chest.

And then I reached between my legs, and my cock was gone. Instead, below the pubic hair, I felt my new moist vagina. That's when I kind of lost it.

"I don't think I want to do this," I said to Luke. "I don't like this and I want you to change me back. Now!"

"James, please," he said soothingly. "It's all right. You will have your penis back when this is finished."

"But it's *gone,*" I said. "I mean, where the fuck is it?"

"It hasn't gone anywhere, James. Your body has merely changed form. Use your mind and your logic. If we can do *this,* we can also restore you."

"Logic? Give me a break, man. You're turning me into a woman with big fake tits and a pussy!"

"Would you like a Xanax?"

"Several!"

I thought he was only making a quip. But he opened the medicine cabinet and took out a dark brown glass pill bottle—not unlike the one that had contained Eva Braun's diet pills.

"These are actually much better than Xanax," he said, pouring one into his palm. "They'll both soothe your nerves and give you a slight sense of euphoria. Which might come in handy, given what lies ahead."

I held out my hand—Patti's hand—and took the tablet. "Is it OK to drink this water?" I asked.

He shrugged. "Doesn't matter."

I put the tablet in my mouth and gulped water from the showerhead to wash it down.

"By the way," Luke said, "you're done. You can step out of the shower at any time. The transformation is complete."

I shut off the tap and stepped out, and Luke handed me a towel. As I dried off, I stepped over to the wood-framed full-length mirror, well knowing what I'd see. It was still a jolt.

There I was. Rather, there *she* was. I was looking at a naked Patti Grant. Besides her Barbie body, I had her face: her collagen-puffed lips, unnaturally white, capped teeth, sculpted nose, and implanted cheeks. I had her bright, empty blue eyes, her long, streaked-blond hair.

I have to say, unlike some gay men who *are* female-identified, I've never wished that I'd been born a woman. And yet that's suddenly what I was.

"This is strange," I said to Luke. And my own words startled me. Because they were in Patti Grant's breathy, sex-kitten voice.

"You came out well," Luke said. "I have no doubt you'll fool God. And his minions."

"I'd fool myself if I didn't know the truth," I said, still in Patti's voice. And that wasn't all that had changed. My *syntax* had become hers as well. "This is so weird. I mean, it's really kind of spooky. How do you guys do this?"

"Jesus *did* perform miracles. He taught us a few tricks."

I pulled on the black lace panties Luke handed me. Then I slipped on a tight red T-shirt that emphasized my nipples. At that point, Luke opened the door so the others could see me.

"Excellent," Deneuve said.

"Yes, very good," Judas said. "When God sees you he will feel a stirring in his loins for the first time in several millennia."

"Indeed," Peter said, his eyes devouring my breasts. "It's too bad we can't 'party down' with you first, as you put it on Earth."

"That's not part of the bargain," I said. "Don't you men get any funny ideas. I *am* a woman of principle, despite what the tabloids say."

Judas clapped. "Perfect! Perfect! The voice! The words! Everything!"

Deneuve handed me the skimpy denim shorts I was to wear. "We have no time for banter. We must move."

While Deneuve helped me into my high heels, Judas used an odd device that resembled a Victorian telephone. That is, it was built into the wall and made of wood, and it had a rotary dial and what looked like a classic earpiece. But there was no mouthpiece, nothing to speak into. And he held it to his temple, not his ear.

After a short time, he "hung up." And he said, "They bought it. God will be expecting you in 20 minutes."

"I don't get it," I said, sounding as dim as Patti. "What is that thing?"

"A telepaphone," Deneuve said. "He called God's house, pretending to be the tracer. Telling them he had found Grant. So now the stage is set. The coach will take you there. It's not far. You remember what to do?"

"Of course," I said with Patti's petulance. "Pull the tube. Jeez, even I can remember *that*."

"Good," said Peter. "We're counting on it."

Deneuve opened the front door, and I saw the coach waiting. "You are on your own from here," she said. "The coach will wait in front of God's house. If all goes well, it will bring you back here. Once God is dead, no one will stop you."

"OK." Patti's voice and the way part of her mind had taken part of mine were actually more unsettling than my appearance.

Deneuve looked deep into my eyes. "You hold the fate of trillions of beings in your hands. Do not fail us, James." Then she added, "Christ, in the vast if shackled power of his spirit, will be with you."

"Gosh, I hope so. This is scary. I mean, I never though I'd have to kill *God* or anything like that."

I shared brief hugs with all of them, which again was odd, feeling my new breasts press against their chests. Then, after final words, I was in the coach. And, as before, almost immediately I reached my destination.

God's house was creepy. Dying oak trees, yellow lawn, dead shrubs, filthy draped windows, cracked and peeling white paint.

A bearded tubbo in a linty black warm-up suit came out to greet me. One of God's bodyguards, I assumed. He opened the coach door for me and said in a slurred voice, "Welcome, Miss Grant. God is expecting you."

I smelled whiskey on his breath.

I followed him into the house, which smelled worse. Mildew and something rotten, like rancid meat. The rooms I caught glimpses of were a mess—cluttered with overdone furniture not unlike the decor at Genesis. And they were littered with earthly brand-name booze bottles and junk food debris. So apparently somewhere in heaven there's a liquor store and a KFC.

The warm-up-clad tub introduced himself as Mike and led me up a stairway to the second floor. From there he took me down a hallway carpeted with dirty blue shag, and along the way we passed several other similar tubbies as well as a thin, wizened old man in a black suit with a black leather bag. He reminded me of William Burroughs.

"That's Dr. Abraham," Mike told me. "He tends the soul infuser."

"The what?"

"It's not important, Miss Grant. But if Dr. Abraham is leaving, that means God must be A-OK. And eager as all get out to meet you. He's been looking forward to this for a long time, ma'am."

"Well," I said, winging it, "I had no idea he wanted to see *me* of all people. I just found out a short time ago. But of course I want to meet God. I mean, gosh, who wouldn't?"

At the end of the hall another burly guard sat by God's door, slumped in an olive-green velvet armchair and reading a Tom Clancy paperback. He pulled himself up as we approached and Mike said to me, "I gotta caution you, Miss Grant, *not* to get God too excited. To be honest, just seeing you is gonna throw him for a loop. Now, I know God is God, so you might be tempted to do whatever he wants. But under no circumstances are you to give him a hand job or anything like that, if you catch my drift. His health is not good, and that could cause some real trouble."

"Sure," I said. "I mean, I guess. But I never even thought that God would want a hand job. I mean—"

"Well, he might. Knowin' God, he might want even more. If that happens, you just call my name. OK? He wants to see you alone, but I'll be right outside the door."

"OK." I touched my heart. "Gosh, I'm so nervous." In truth, I felt calm and focused. The pill, whatever it was, had definitely kicked in.

The guard by the door stepped inside to tell God I'd arrived. In a moment he came back out and said, "He says to send you in."

I stepped through the door, which the guard closed behind me. The room was large and dark, the windows heavily draped. The main light source was the big-screen TV, which was on and faced the king-size, red-velvet-canopied bed where God lay. He was watching, of all things, a rerun of *Gilligan's Island.* I could barely make him out in the dim light: just a figure propped against dirty pillows, breathing with difficulty.

The stench was intense, the reek of ancient urine and feces.

Then God spoke in an old man's voice. "Come closer, my dear. Step into the light."

I took several mincing Patti steps toward his bed, and he switched on a harsh, overhead light that illuminated my protruding breasts.

"Very nice," God said in a phlegmy whisper. "Yes, yes, very tasty. You are even more sexy in death than on the screen, my child. Turn around full circle. Let me see all of you."

I did as asked. I was close enough now to have spotted the translucent tube running from a machine that looked like a prop from a '50s horror flick into his bony white chest. In the brighter light, I saw his face as well. Wrinkled, lipless, and squinty-eyed with a few wisps of white hair on his skull. He looked at least 90 in human years. To be honest, he bore a strong resemblance to Strom Thurmond, minus the orange hair. Or maybe I should say Strom Thurmond bore a strong resemblance to God, except with orange hair.

"Yes, a fine ass," said God, as I turned to give him a full view. "Firm and pert. As perfect as an illustration. Come closer, my child. I won't ask for more than you can give. I only want to touch your flesh. Just touch."

He beckoned me closer with a gnarled, yellow, liver-spotted claw.

This creeped me out, not that I wasn't already creeped out. But it was also my chance to act.

"OK," I said with Patti-like trepidation. "I guess that won't hurt anything. But just for the record, I am not some big slut like some people think."

"I know you're not, my dear," God said. "I know everything there is to know about you. I'm God, after all." He chuckled.

Stepping closer, I saw the soul bubbles moving in a steady stream through the tube taped into his chest. Then...a shot of luck as the action on TV momentarily distracted him. Ginger and Mary Ann on-screen together.

I took the chance and reached for the tube. He saw what I was doing, and our eyes met for just a moment before I yanked the tube from his chest. In that fraction of a second, in his mean scared eyes I saw all the horror and pain in the universe.

He gurgled as the tube poured its slippery soul bubbles onto the floor. He tried to cry out but couldn't catch his breath. His eyes took on the startled look of death. And he fell back against the dirty velvet pillows. I was waiting for him to instantly decompose the way Deneuve had said he would. But instead I blinked and found myself in a sun-drenched Santa Barbara hospital room, looking up at Todd and my mother and father.

My chest hurt like hell.

"Jim?" Todd said. "Can you hear me?"

"Where's God?"

"I think he's playing golf," Todd said.

"No. I killed him."

I saw my mom exchange a look of concern with my dad.

"Do you know who I am?" Todd asked.

"Of course. You're Todd. Should I tell you the year and who's president too?"

"Wouldn't hurt."

"Nineteen fifty-three. Eisenhower."

"Very funny," Todd said. "Do you remember what happened to you?"

"Where? Here or there?"

"Where's there?" Todd said.

I hesitated. "I'll tell you later. I remember being shot, if that's what you're asking."

"Yes, you were shot, honey," my mom said. "We were worried you weren't going to make it."

"I wasn't worried. Catherine Deneuve told me I'd make it."

"Who?" my dad said.

Todd intervened. "Maybe you *should* save it for later."

"Probably," I said, reaching to check out my body, despite the incredible pain the movement caused. And it *was* my body. No breasts. I felt between my legs. My cock had a catheter stuck in it, but it was there. "Thank God," I said.

"What?" my dad said.

"Nothing. I'm hurting. I need some Demerol."

Todd rang for the nurse. I quaked when she arrived. She looked enough like Catherine Deneuve to have been her twin.

Eventually I told Todd the full story of my *experience.* He listened quietly as I laid it all out, nodding in a neutral manner until I was done. Then he said, "I think you were probably dreaming or hallucinating or whatever."

"That's definitely a possibility," I said.

"You were unconscious for six days. But maybe on some level you were conscious. I mean, that nurse did look an awful lot like Catherine Deneuve."

I couldn't help but think of Dorothy from *The Wizard of Oz.* "And you were there. And you were there. And you too, Catherine Deneuve."

"And your parents and I discussed what happened at the mission ad nauseam. Which is probably how you knew what went down after you got shot."

"Could be," I said. "It's logical. But maybe they arranged it this way so I'd question if it really happened the way I remember. Or so if I wrote about all of this, which I'm going to do, other people would question it."

"Enough already."

I let it go.

As it turns out, the Germans lied about cutting off Vera Henderson's head. I guess that was their idea of a joke. Once they realized she wasn't my mother, they tied her up and gagged her and left her in her duplex. She was badly shaken but otherwise unharmed.

My mother, understandably, was afraid to go back to the duplex, fearing both a return visit from the Germans and the Genesis cadre. This latter fear was not unfounded, despite the demise of Gene and his two pals at the mission—in fact, *because* of the demise of Gene and his two pals. If any of them had survived, the FBI might have been able to gain evidence that Michael had ordered the attack. As it is, Genesis is very much on the feds' radar, and I understand that many of Michael's followers have left the fold. But that doesn't mean there aren't still loyal minions seeking revenge.

In case you're wondering, my parents are back together. The shared trauma of what happened that Saturday apparently sped up the process of reconciliation that was already well under way. For obvious reasons, I won't tell you where they're living.

Somewhat amazingly, a similar rapprochement has taken place between my father and me. In truth, he *has* changed. He'll never be liberal. There will always be vast chasms of political disagreement between us. But he *has* made a major shift in his feelings about gay people, again, a process already well under way thanks to my mother and greatly accelerated by the events of that Saturday. To be exact, it was hard for him not to be grateful to Todd, who'd shot the second Genesis bot at the mission just as the guy was drawing a bead on my dad, thereby saving my dad's life in the great heroic tradition of masculine gunfights.

Todd and I have moved as well. For the same reasons as my parents: Baldur Schenk's people are very likely still looking for revenge, and Michael and his nekkid fundie freak show are definitely still looking for revenge. I won't tell you where we live, except to say that it's quite pleasant and we're near the water. We're using different names, and we've taken some steps to change our physical appearances, short of plastic surgery. Still, even my oldest friends, when I've seen them, have been initially fooled. Same with Todd and his friends.

We feel as safe as we're ever going to feel. And we don't live in fear.

By the way, we've scrapped the Bud Chaswell tape. As it turns out, the tape wasn't needed to bring down Chaswell. His wife, of all people, did it for us. Apparently she'd known of Ed Keck's gay past, accepted it, and grown to care for him a great deal. And she didn't like the way her husband had treated Ed after his arrest, and she went public with it. On *Larry King* she said, "I understood why Bud had to relieve Ed of his duties as president of the alliance. Given the nature of the charges, Bud had to cut his losses. But I will never understand why my husband said what he did to Ed on the phone, moments before Ed took his own life."

"And what was that?" asked Larry.

"He said...he said, 'Jump.' "

Bud Chaswell, of course, still has his backers, people who would've said exactly the same thing to Ed. But his power base is greatly eroded, and all but the most rabidly right-wing politicians have distanced themselves from him.

After that, we decided to destroy Revelations once and for all. I mean, maybe my near-death experience was, as Todd suggested, a hallucination. But maybe it wasn't. Maybe an insane God really is dead, and a beneficent Christ has taken over. I like to think so, anyway. And if that's the case, there's no need for Revelations.

Oh, yeah, the Juice tape. We sent it to Brigitte's riot grrrl pals in San Francisco. They loved it.

Editor's Note
I Never Met the Man

I never met James Robert Baker. After a lifelong battle with depression, he committed suicide on November 5, 1997. This less than two months before I moved to the Los Angeles area—Baker's home turf—to become associate publisher and editor in chief at Alyson Books.

At the time of his death, Baker was the author of four critically acclaimed novels, all of which were inexplicably out of print in the United States: *Adrenaline,* a homo roman noir (written under the pseudonym James Dillinger); *Fuel Injected Dreams,* a rock-and-roll antinostalgia tale about a reclusive, demented genius record producer turned necrophiliac; *Boy Wonder,* a satiric mock oral history about a crazed, obsessive filmmaker; and *Tim and Pete*, a homo love story-anarchist tract. (*Adrenaline* and *Tim and Pete* have since been reissued.)

Baker was also renown for his underground film work. (He attended UCLA's film school, where he won the prestigious Samuel Goldwyn Screenwriting Award.) His first film, *Mouse Klub Konfidential,* about a Mouseketeer turned gay bondage pornographer, scandalized the 1976 San Francisco Gay and Lesbian film festival. And his second film, *Blonde Death,* about patricide in Orange County, Calif., became a cult favorite. Like his books, though, his films were unavailable to the general public.

Baker had an obvious love-hate relationship with

Hollywood. He wanted to see his work on-screen, yet at the same time he despised nearly everything about the Hollywood system. In a *Los Angeles Times* interview, he once described film executives as "rabid, hideous morons" and said of his experience in the film world, "I felt like a door-to-door salesman going to all these pitch meetings." But of course he never forgot his cinematic roots. All of his books, including *Anarchy,* are laced with film references. And never has anyone so thoroughly skewered Hollywood as Baker, most specifically in his magnum opus, *Boy Wonder:* Baker's Shark Trager makes Michael Tolkin's Griffin Mill (*The Player*) look like Beaver Cleaver.

I initially became acquainted with Baker's work shortly after my arrival at Alyson when his agent, Joshua Bilmes, asked if I'd be interested in looking at an unpublished novel by the recently deceased author of *Tim and Pete.* I hadn't read *Tim and Pete,* but I had seen several rave reviews, so I agreed to consider the new work.

Shortly thereafter, a manuscript titled *Testosterone* arrived—a well-written, well-plotted, nicely polished tale of obsession, compulsive sex, and revenge. I loved it. I happily bought the rights and asked if there was anything more that Bilmes could send. There was. In addition to copies of Baker's four out-of-print books, I received a large pile of other unpublished writing.

Among this unpublished material was a wild, unstructured,

at times incoherent manuscript titled *Mean Beach.* The manuscript was 500 pages of closely spaced type—more than twice the length of *Testosterone*—and it seemed to lack any sort of tangible plot. In short, it was a mess. I quickly reached the conclusion that it was neither publishable nor salvageable. Consequently, *Mean Beach* was shelved, along with another manuscript, *Crucifying Todd,* which appeared to be an early and very messy draft of *Testosterone*.

At the time, I suspected *Mean Beach* was probably what Baker had been working on near the very end of his life, right before his suicide. It contrasted so sharply with the brilliantly taut *Testosterone* that such timing seemed the only logical conclusion. Especially after reading his other works, all of which are utterly spellbinding and all of which, with the exception of *Boy Wonder* (which I consider an *intentional* ramble), are among the most tightly woven books ever written.

Somehow, though, *Mean Beach* got under my skin. I couldn't shake it. So I read the manuscript a second time. Parts of it were spectacular and desperately deserved to see the light of day. But still, I couldn't see how the manuscript would ever become publishable. So I read it again, this time taking detailed notes. (I'm nothing if not stubborn.) It was in reading and rereading those notes that I finally began to see what sort of monster Baker had created: a black comedy. Very black. Blacker than black. A whole new subspecies of black.

I began to formulate, from the notes I'd taken, a workable plot. I did so by working backward, asking, "What is the end of this story?" The answer was obvious: The penultimate scene is when the protagonist meets Catherine Deneuve and kills God. (Interestingly, this is the only one of Baker's books where he uses himself as the protagonist.) I later spoke with Ron Robertson, Baker's surviving life partner, telling him I hoped to rework the manuscript, and he confirmed my conclusion about the conclusion, saying, "Whatever you do, don't cut the scene with Catherine Deneuve. That's the best part."

I did, however, cut other scenes with wild abandon, drawing big red lines through entire pages of the notes I'd taken, paring the tale down to only what drove the story toward its inevitable end. (The largest chunk to disappear from the original draft is a second trip to Europe, this one on a private party plane with a David Geffen-like media mogul. This trip involves an affairette with a female folksinger, a run-in with her psychotic boyfriend, an encounter with Vlad in the loo at the Louvre, a planned suicide gone awry, and real tears from one of Judy Garland's children. All of which in no way advanced the plot except to leave James penniless in Madison, Wis.) From those heavily red-inked notes an outline was developed, and within a month I'd compiled a new draft of *Mean Beach,* which by then I'd retitled *Anarchy.*

I hope fans of Baker will not notice a difference in the style of prose between *Anarchy* and his other books. In reworking the text I referred often to the original pages, altering my own prose to fit Baker's language and word choices as much as possible. In doing so, I found that my own writing style is substantially similar to Baker's. At times almost eerily so: I would type a scene, compare it to the original, and find that the text matched almost word for word. The further along I got, the more frequent this became.

Nevertheless, I did have to substantially alter sections of text and plot. A good example is the aforementioned landing of James in Madison with absolutely no resources. And I admit that the cultural references in the book are sometimes Baker's, sometimes mine. I won't tell which are mine and which are his, though I will say that one movie reference was put in for my friend Angela "Wiener Dog" Brown, another for my friend Christopher "Montese" Horan. They'll recognize which ones are theirs. Otherwise I'll disown them.

I would like to thank my editor, Angela Brown, for her skillful blue pen and for being a wonderful friend. (Yes, I realize the back cover says "Edited by Scott Brassart," but somebody had to edit me, and that person was Angela.) I would also like to thank Joshua Bilmes for introducing me to the work of James Robert Baker, and Ron Robertson for working so hard to keep the memory of James Robert Baker alive. Finally, I would like to thank James Robert Baker for being who he was and writing what he did. I am honored to have my name linked with his. I only wish I'd met him.

Scott Brassart
Los Angeles, 2002